PUFFIN BOOKS

THE JEAN LITTLE COLLECTION

JEAN LITTLE is the author of more than twenty books for children, including *Mama's Going to Buy You a Mockingbird, Mine for Keeps,* and *His Banner Over Me.* Among her many awards for her work is the Mr. Christie Award for *Willow and Twig.* Her books have been translated into French, German, Dutch, Danish, Norwegian, Greek and Japanese. Jean Little lives in Elora, Ontario.

The Jean Little Collection

Different Dragons

Lost and Found

One to Grow On

Puffin Books

PUFFIN BOOKS
Published by the Penguin Group
Penguin Books Canada Ltd, 10 Alcorn Avenue,
Toronto, Ontario, Canada M4V 3B2
Penguin Books Ltd, 80 Strand, London WC2R 0RL, England
Penguin Putnam Inc., 375 Hudson Street, New York, New York 10014, U.S.A.
Penguin Books Australia Ltd, Ringwood, Victoria, Australia
Penguin Books (NZ) Ltd, cnr Rosedale and Airborne Roads, Albany,
Auckland 1310, New Zealand

Penguin Books Ltd, Registered Offices: Harmondsworth, Middlesex, England

Different Dragons first published in Penguin by Penguin Books Canada, 1986.
Published in Puffin Books, 1988.

Lost and Found first published in Puffin by Penguin Books Canada, 1985.

One to Grow On first published by Little, Brown & Company, 1969.
Published in Puffin Books, 1991.

First published in one volume as *The Jean Little Collection* in
Puffin Books, 2001

1 3 5 7 9 10 8 6 4 2

Publisher's note: This book is a work of fiction. Names, characters, places and incidents either are the product of the author's imagination or are used fictitiously, and any resemblance to actual persons living or dead, events, or locales is entirely coincidental.

Manufactured in Canada.

NATIONAL LIBRARY OF CANADA CATALOGUING IN PUBLICATION DATA

Little, Jean, 1932–
The Jean Little collection

Contents: One to grow on — Lost and found — Different dragons.

ISBN 0-14-131372-2

CCLI. Title. II. Title: Lost and found. III. Title: One to grow on.
IV. Title: Different dragons.

PS8523.I77J42 2001 jC813'.54 C2001-901745-6
PZ7.L7225Je 2001

Visit Penguin Canada's website at **www.penguin.ca**

Contents

Different Dragons

Contents

CHAPTER ONE

Not That Kind of Boy

"Wake up, Ben," Dad said. "We'll be there soon."

Ben Tucker was not really asleep. He heard what his father said. But he stayed slumped down as far as his seatbelt would let him. He kept his eyes shut. If he woke up, they would be almost at Aunt Rose's house. Maybe, if he kept very still and did not open his eyes, Dad would change his mind and take him back home.

"Benjamin Tucker," Ben's father said, "don't you want to see the house I lived in when I was your age?"

Ben did want to see it. He had heard so much about the big old stone house in Guelph, where his father and his uncle and aunt had lived when they were kids. He just did not want to have to stay in it, not without Mum and Dad and Jimmy. He didn't even know Aunt Rose. Oh, he had met her.

She had come to visit them in Vancouver. But that had been ages ago, when he was little. He couldn't even remember what she looked like.

Maybe she hated kids. Jimmy said she did. He had laughed when he said it, but it might be true. Jimmy ought to know. He was six years older than Ben was, and a lot bigger. And Jimmy had visited Aunt Rose last summer, when she lived away up in Hearst.

Now Aunt Rose had moved back into the old family home which had been rented for years. She was having part of the upstairs turned into an apartment. She had asked Ben's family to come for a visit before the apartment was rented. Right now she had lots of spare rooms. Ben would have been happy to go with his family, but that was not what was going to happen. He was to go there first, on his own, and the rest were not coming until suppertime on Sunday.

It was Dad's idea. He said it was Ben's turn to go somewhere without the rest of them. He said Ben would enjoy it. Jimmy was going to stay with a friend he'd made at camp last summer. And Dad and Mum had signed up to go to some dumb weekend conference.

So Ben was to stay at Aunt Rose's by himself. He had told them he didn't want to go, but they didn't care. Dad just said it would be good for him. Ben had never guessed that Dad could be so mean. How could they make him stay with this stranger for a whole weekend! This was only Friday. How was he going to get through the hours and hours until the others came? He would be there without anyone he knew for two whole days and two whole nights!

"Hey," Dad tried again. "I asked you a question. Aren't you speaking to me?"

Still pretending not to hear, Ben squeezed his eyes more tightly shut. That made two big tears roll out and slide down his cheeks. He gave a sad little sniff, too. There. That would let Dad know how he was feeling.

"Oh, Ben, don't start that again," Mr. Tucker said. He sounded tired. "You're too big to be such a crybaby. You're going to have a wonderful time. Your Aunt Rose knows what boys like."

"She can't know," Ben muttered. "She hasn't any boys."

"So what? She does know. She writes books for boys, remember. Not every boy has a writer for an aunt. It will be exciting for you having this chance to get to know her. You ought to be proud. You are going to visit a real live author. Think of that!"

Big deal, Ben thought. Was there such a thing as an unreal live author? Would he still have to go if she were a real dead one? He almost grinned but stopped himself in time. He didn't want Dad to catch him smiling.

"Tell the truth," Dad coaxed. "Aren't you really looking forward to meeting her? You must at least be curious."

Ben was. He couldn't help it. He was proud, too. He had seen Aunt Rose's books in the bookstore and in the library at school. Mum had read some of them out loud to him. They were great books, filled with magical adventures. When his teacher, Miss Morris, had heard he was going to see his famous aunt as soon as school ended, she had asked Ben to get her autograph. Some of the other kids had been jealous.

"You are a lucky boy," Miss Morris had said, "having Rose Tucker for an aunt."

Ben had felt lucky then. But not now. He wished Dad would stop trying to talk him around. Even if every single thing he said was true, Ben was not going to feel happy about this visit.

"Her books are all about boys who run away from home to fight dragons and find treasure. I'm not that kind of boy. She won't like me," he burst out, his voice shaking.

Dad did not say anything for a long moment. When he did answer, his words startled Ben.

"Everybody has to fight a dragon sometime," he said slowly. "You have different dragons to fight, that's all. I think you might even slay one or two this weekend."

Ben stared at his father. Had he gone crazy? Was Aunt Rose a dragon? Was that what he meant? No. It must be some dumb grown-up joke.

"Rose is really glad you are coming," Dad said. "She told me so herself. She'll show you all around the old house. When we come, you'll be the expert. You'll get ahead of your big brother for once. Maybe you'll have so much fun that you won't want Sunday afternoon to come."

Ben jerked around and glared at his father. "I will not have a good time," he yelled. At a look from Dad, he stopped shouting, but he kept on talking fast. "Why can't I go with you and Mum? Jimmy says Aunt Rose is really mean."

Mr. Tucker sighed. He took a deep breath.

"If your brother did say that, you know he was only teasing. You also know why you can't come with us. We've told you often enough. We are going to a conference. No children will be there. Your mother and I have not been away for a whole weekend by ourselves since you were a baby. If we don't go soon, we'll be too old to travel."

Ben knew that his father was kidding. He and Mum were old but not that old. Dad was trying to make him smile. But Ben didn't feel like smiling. He turned his head away and looked out the window.

Dad pulled off to the side of the road. He stopped the car and shifted so that he could look at Ben. Gently he drew Ben around so that they faced each other. When he spoke, his voice was deep and serious.

"Ben, you're old enough now to start thinking of somebody besides yourself," he said. "Don't you think Mum deserves a holiday?"

Ben squirmed. That was a trick question. If he said she did, Dad would think that everything was all right. It wasn't. Why couldn't Mum think about him instead? He knew better than to say that out loud. So he just sat there and said nothing at all. That was the only safe thing to do.

Dad spoke sharply for the first time.

"Whether you like it or not, you are going to stay at Rose's for a couple of days," he snapped. "If you have made up your mind to be miserable, you probably will be. If you make the best of it instead, you'll enjoy yourself. That's up to you. But stop sulking. Grow up, Ben."

Ben's chin came up with a jerk. He bit his lip to keep it from trembling. But he couldn't make any words come out because of the big lump in his throat.

Maybe Dad guessed. He gave Ben's knee a comforting squeeze and spoke more gently. "I want you to try an experiment, Benjamin Tucker. Do you think you could at least try to have a good time at Rose's? I think you might surprise yourself if you'll only try."

Ben knew it wouldn't work. He was going to have a terrible time. He thought of what his brother Jimmy had really said. "She won't let you keep the hall light on like a baby," he had jeered.

Had Jimmy only been teasing? Ben could not always tell when he was fooling and when he wasn't.

Dad reached into his pocket. He pulled out one of his big handkerchiefs and handed it to Ben. Ben wiped his eyes.

"How about it?" Mr. Tucker asked. "Will you give it a try?"

"Okay. I'll try," Ben said in a small, husky voice. Dad gave him a big smile. It changed his face so much that Ben blinked. Had his father really been worried about him? It looked like it.

"Good for you, Ben." His father started the car up again. "I was talking to Rose on the phone last night," he said as he drove. "I wasn't going to say anything, but it might help. She told me she has a big surprise for you, something you will really like, I'll bet. She didn't say what it was, but it must be something pretty special."

Ben felt better. A surprise for him! Did that mean a present?

Suddenly the car turned into a driveway.

"Here we are," Dad said. "And there's Rose in the garden."

Ben gulped. He grabbed his father's arm and held on tight.

"Promise you'll come as soon as you can on Sunday. And that you won't not come, no matter what," he begged.

"We'll be here in time for supper if we have to hire a plane," his father promised.

CHAPTER TWO

Aunt Rose

Ben got out of the car slowly. His stomach felt as though it was doing flip-flops. He was scared to look at Aunt Rose. He knew without turning to look that his aunt was coming across the grass to meet them. Dad hurried toward her without waiting for Ben.

"Hello, stranger," Aunt Rose said.

She didn't really mean Dad was a stranger. You wouldn't hug a stranger the way she was hugging his father.

"Stranger yourself," Dad said, laughing and hugging her back. "I'd have known you anywhere, fat as you are."

That made Ben stop looking at the ground. He stared at his aunt, instead. He remembered her right away. She was not a total stranger, after all. She was not fat, either. Dad must be kidding. She was tall, almost as tall as Ben's father. She had short fair hair, only a little darker than Ben's. And

her eyes were smiling at him over Dad's shoulder.

As his father let go of her and turned to draw him forward, Ben stood as tall as he could. He did not smile. He even frowned a little. He had a feeling that if he smiled back at this aunt of his, she might kiss him. Ben did not want to be kissed, not by somebody he didn't know, even if he did remember her face now.

Maybe she guessed how he felt. She came toward him, still smiling, and just stood and looked at him for a moment. Then she spoke.

"Hi, Tommy," she said.

Ben scowled. He hated being called Tommy. Grown-ups thought it was cute because of that dumb poem about Little Tommy Tucker. Ben and Jimmy agreed that the poem was soppy and being called Tommy Tucker made them both feel like dopes. No wonder Jimmy hadn't liked Aunt Rose if she was that kind of grown up!

Then Aunt Rose burst out laughing.

"I'm sorry, Ben," she said. "I just wanted to see if you would make the same disgusted face your father always made when people called him Tommy. You do, exactly the same. You look so much like him when he was your age, too. I promise never to call you that again."

Ben couldn't help smiling back then. He liked it when people said he looked like Dad. And she did sound sorry. Maybe Jimmy had only been teasing when he had said she was mean.

He couldn't think of what to say. Perhaps she guessed that. She turned back to talk with his father as they started up the front steps of the big old house.

The house seemed strange to Ben. For one thing, it was made of stone. In Vancouver there weren't any stone houses. It was a tall house, too. Ben's home was all on one floor, but this house had three big windows upstairs. There were two more wide windows, one on each side of the front door. The door was double, like the windows, with a brass knocker on each side. It was all so big that Ben could hardly believe his eyes.

Was there an attic? He craned his neck looking for any sign of one. He had never been in a house with an attic, but this one was so huge that it ought to have one. In Aunt Rose's first book, a boy found a secret treasure hidden in an attic. Ben couldn't see any tiny cobwebby windows up under the eaves, but maybe they were on the other side of the house.

"Come on, Ben, stop dreaming," Dad said. "We're waiting for you."

Ben jumped. He felt his face getting red. He ran up the steps and in through the big front door Dad was holding open for him.

He stared around the shadowy front hall. It was

spooky. Then he saw the banister Dad had told them about. You could slide down it or you could straddle the flat round part at the bottom and pretend you were riding a horse. Neat!

"Have you time for a cup of coffee before you go, John?" Aunt Rose was asking.

Ben's stomach tightened. Dad glanced at his watch.

"I really should be leaving," he began.

Then he looked down at Ben's hand, clutching his sleeve.

"I guess I can spare ten minutes. If you show us where you're putting Ben, I can help get him settled."

"I've put Ben in my old room," Aunt Rose said. "Let's go up the back stairs."

Ben followed her. He carried the small suitcase with his clothes inside. He thought he looked grown-up, but he was glad Dad was right behind him.

The back stairs opened out of the kitchen. They were steep and narrow and a bit dark. Ben had never been in a house with two sets of stairs before. These stairs had walls on both sides instead of a banister. If he lived here, Ben thought he would use the front stairs.

"This way," his aunt said, opening a door. "You get to choose, Ben, whether you want to sleep up or down."

Ben stared at the bunks. He had never slept in a bunk bed. The top one had a neat ladder going up to it, but it looked very high in the air. Ben liked the bottom bunk better. It would be like having his own little cave. Would they think he was a sissy if he took the bottom one? He searched Dad's face.

"Well, which will it be?" his father asked, smiling. He was leaving it up to Ben. And Jimmy wasn't here to make fun of him.

"I'd rather sleep in the bottom one," he said in a low voice.

"Fine," Aunt Rose said. "Jimmy chose the bottom bunk when he stayed with me last summer. He said he was scared he'd roll out of the top one, although nobody has fallen out of it yet. There's a light right here at the head, which you can turn on when you want to read. I think that's what Jimmy really liked."

Ben gazed at the bed light. If he got scared in the dark, all he had to do was reach up and turn it on. And Jimmy had been scared. Jimmy!

"It's great," he breathed.

He put his bag down on top of the bed. He undid it. Then, as he opened it, he saw his pajamas right on top. He swallowed.

"How about that cup of coffee, Rose?" Dad said all at once. "Ben can explore up here later."

"You'll have to settle for instant coffee if you're in such a rush."

"Instant will be fine," Ben's father said, following her out of the room and down the stairs.

Ben ran after him and caught hold of his hand.

"Don't tell Mum I'm going to sleep in a bunk bed," he said. "Let me show her on Sunday."

Dad grinned down at him.

"I won't say a word about it," he promised. "You'll have a lot to tell us when we get here."

He drank his coffee standing up.

"I really do have to go now," he said, heading for the front door. "We have to be at the conference by eight o'clock. You behave, Ben. See that he does, Rose. It's good of you to have him on his own like this."

"I'm glad to have him to myself," Aunt Rose said, putting one hand lightly on Ben's shoulder. "We'll get to know each other better without the rest of you getting in our way. Have a wonderful time, John. Drive carefully."

Dad gave them both a quick hug. Ben felt tears coming into his eyes. If Dad didn't go fast, he knew he was going to cry.

Dad must have known. He ran down the front steps, jumped into the car, waved once and was gone.

Ben wanted to run after the car and shout at his

father to come back. But then he heard Aunt Rose's voice.

"Ben Tucker," she said, "what do you like best of all to eat?"

He turned slowly and looked at her. He was so surprised that he stopped wanting to cry. "If it isn't too, too complicated, you and I could make it for supper," she said. "Just don't say Baked Alaska or chocolate eclairs. I tried those once and they tasted terrible."

Ben did like chocolate eclairs, but they weren't his favourite thing. He had never heard of Baked Alaska.

"I like spaghetti best," he said at last. His voice shook a little and he had to rub away some tears with the back of his hand. His aunt did not seem to notice.

"What a relief!" she cried. "I'm a great cook when it comes to spaghetti. You'll have to help, though, and make sure I do it just the way you like it. I have a pumpkin pie for dessert. Do you like pumpkin pie?"

Ben grinned. "Is there whipped cream?"

"There will be when you whip it," his aunt said.

A bunk bed. A light he could turn on whenever he wanted. Spaghetti, just the way he liked it. Pumpkin pie with whipped cream for supper and the surprise yet to come! Thinking of all these things, Ben felt much better. Aunt Rose was nice, too, not a bit like a dragon.

"I like lots of sauce and lots of cheese," he told her, "and I like little meatballs, with no onions in them."

His aunt leaned down all at once and kissed him on top of his head.

"No onions, on my word of honour," she said.

Being kissed wasn't all that bad.

CHAPTER THREE

The Surprise

"I have a surprise for you," Aunt Rose said. "I hope you'll like it. But we'd better get started on our cooking or we won't be ready when it arrives."

"What is the surprise?" Ben asked, trotting after her as she led the way to the kitchen.

"If I told you that, it wouldn't be a surprise, would it?"

"I guess not," Ben had to admit. "When will it . . . be here?"

"About seven-thirty," his aunt said. "Do you think you can wait till then?"

Ben nodded politely, but it did seem a long time to wait. It was just five o'clock now.

"I'll keep you busy. Then the time will go faster. You can start by whipping the cream for the pie."

Ben had never whipped cream before. At home he and Jimmy helped with the dishes, but they hardly ever got to cook. Whipping cream wasn't hard to do, though. He had watched his mother do it millions of times. It was simple.

"Do you know how?" Aunt Rose asked as she got out a bowl, the carton of whipping cream, some sugar and the bottle of vanilla.

"Sure," Ben said. He did know how. He was sure he did. You beat the cream first. Then you put in the sugar and vanilla at the end. It was a cinch.

Aunt Rose was busy filling a big pot with water. That would be for the spaghetti. She wasn't even watching him. He dumped the cream into the bowl, stuck the beaters in, turned them on and began to whip.

He felt great, standing there, in charge of the whirring electric mixer. He flicked the switch from Medium to High and back again. He beat and beat the cream. All at once, it began to get thicker.

Ben turned the beaters off and looked at it. It seemed about right. He'd better be sure to beat it enough, though. He turned the beaters on again.

"That must be about done," Aunt Rose said over her shoulder.

"Just about," Ben said. He kept on beating. Then he turned the beaters off and looked at the cream again.

It was full of queer little yellowish flecks.

Ben stared down at it. Should he tell Aunt Rose?

He didn't want to. Maybe once he beat in the sugar and vanilla, it would be all right. That was probably what it needed.

Ben measured out a couple of spoonfuls of sugar. He dumped them in. Then, with the greatest care, he added the vanilla. Feeling nervous, he switched the beaters on once more.

Aunt Rose turned to look at him.

"Be careful, Ben, or you'll whip it to butter," she warned.

Ben's heart sank. He peered into the bowl, hoping against hope that the bits of yellow would have disappeared. They were bigger. He *had* whipped the cream to butter. He stood very still, his head hanging. How was he going to tell his aunt?

"Benjamin Tucker, don't look like that," Aunt Rose said. "The sky hasn't fallen. What's wrong? *Did* you whip it to butter?"

She sounded as though she were laughing. Ben felt awful. His aunt came and stood beside him. She looked down at what he had done.

"I've always wondered how pumpkin pie would taste with butter on it," she said. She was really laughing now.

"I'm sorry," Ben said miserably. "I thought I knew how." His voice trailed off. The ache was back in his throat.

He looked up. Aunt Rose's eyes were twinkling

down at him. He gazed at the blobs of butter and did his best to smile.

"Don't worry, Ben," Aunt Rose said, putting the bowl in the fridge. "I've done the same thing myself. I think we'll make this into sweet butter and eat it with muffins some other time. I have some more whipping cream I was going to use tomorrow. If at first you don't succeed . . ."

This time, Ben stopped whipping at exactly the right moment. Supper was delicious. He had two helpings of spaghetti. He wanted to have more pie, too, but he didn't have any room left.

While they did the dishes, Aunt Rose told him funny stories about when she and Dad were kids.

"What is your bedtime?" she asked when they had finished.

"Nine o'clock on weekends," Ben told her.

The thought of going to bed here, even in the neat bunk bed with his own light, made Ben feel lonesome again.

"How about a game of Snakes and Ladders?" Aunt Rose said quickly. Ben didn't think much of Snakes and Ladders. He wondered if she had Monopoly. Before he could make up his mind whether it would be rude to ask, the doorbell chimed.

"The surprise has arrived!" Aunt Rose said, going to answer the door. Ben was right on her heels. But when they got to the front hall, he heard

something outside the door making a lot of noise. Whatever the surprise was, it banged and thumped and scratched.

Ben felt uneasy, all at once. He drew back.

Then Aunt Rose pulled open the door. In shot a very tall man gripping a leash. At the end of the leash was an enormous, cream coloured dog with floppy golden ears. The dog made straight for Ben. He was a Labrador retriever. To Ben he looked as big as a lion.

Ben screamed and ducked behind Aunt Rose. He hated dogs even more than he hated the dark. Dogs were dangerous. They jumped at you and knocked you down and bit you. Sometimes they even killed people. One of the kids had brought a story to school about somebody being attacked by a savage dog and nearly dying. Miss Morris had said they shouldn't trust strange dogs. When a large stray had got into the school one day, she had kept the door of their classroom shut until she was sure it was gone. She wouldn't even let anybody go to the bathroom.

"It might be vicious," she had said.

Mum and Dad said it was foolish to be so afraid of dogs. But Miss Morris had been scared. And she was a teacher!

"He won't hurt you," the man half shouted over the racket the huge dog's paws were making. "Labs are friendly. He's young and foolish but he's harmless, honest. He gets very excited still when he goes visiting and he likes boys. He just wants to play. Stop it, Gully, you idiot! His name is Gully. It's short for Gulliver Gallivant."

Ben did not care what the monster's name was. He had both arms wound tightly around Aunt Rose from behind. He wished she were a tree so he could climb up her. He was shaking so hard his teeth chattered.

Aunt Rose reached around and tried to pull him loose. He hid his face against her back and hung on for dear life.

"You'd better shut Gully in the kitchen for now, Bob," she said at last. "I should have told Ben what was coming and let him get used to the idea first. John said that he was frightened of dogs, but I didn't take it seriously. Gully is such a lamb. But maybe he does take getting used to."

The man looked worried. Gully was pulling hard on the leash. His tail was thwacking against the man's leg. It sounded like a whip to Ben.

"I'm sorry I didn't know sooner," Bob said. "I could have made other plans for Gully."

"Don't be silly," Aunt Rose told him. "Put Gully in the kitchen now and run along. As soon as Ben sees how gentle the dog is, they'll make friends in no time."

Make friends with a dog? Never!

Ben could hear Bob dragging Gully across the room. Gully did not want to go out to the kitchen. Bob had to pull hard. Once he got him there, he spoke in a loud, firm voice.

"Gulliver, stay!"

Then he shut the kitchen door.

Ben held his breath and listened. Would Gully charge right through the closed door? He didn't. He whimpered. Then Ben could hear him running around, exploring the kitchen.

Bob came back. Ben had loosened his grip on his aunt and was now peering around her. The tall man gave him a troubled smile.

"Hi, Ben," he said. "I'm Bob Wells. My wife and I live just up the block. I'm sorry our surprise has been such a flop. But you'll like Gully when you get to know him. You'll have to help Rose look after him. He's staying for the weekend, too. Rose, I left the bag with his stuff on top of your fridge."

Aunt Rose pulled Ben in front of her. Now, keeping one arm around him, she sank down on the nearest chair.

"Ben, don't be so silly," she said. "Gully hasn't a mean bone in his body. Did you see how beautiful he is?"

Ben shook his head. He would not meet her

eyes. He did not think Gulliver was beautiful. He thought he was horrible. Maybe *he* was the dragon Dad had talked about. If he was, he'd be the one to slay Ben, if he got the chance. That dog probably ate a couple of boys every day for breakfast.

"Well, I've got to get going," Bob said, when Ben made no answer. "Goodbye, Rose, and good luck."

Once the front door shut behind him, Aunt Rose and Ben stared at each other. Then Aunt Rose began to laugh again. That made Ben mad. This wasn't like whipping the cream to butter. This was serious. Ben wanted to go home right away.

"Can he stay in the kitchen till Sunday?" he asked.

"He can stay there till you're in bed, anyway," his aunt said. "Tomorrow will be soon enough for you to make friends."

Ben did not argue. If he started talking about how he felt, he'd cry. And he was not going to cry in front of this aunt who kept laughing over nothing.

"Can I go to bed now?" he said.

Aunt Rose glanced at her watch.

"It's only eight o'clock," she told him. "You said your bedtime wasn't till nine. Wouldn't you like to play a game? Or I could read to you, if you'd rather."

Ben looked down at his feet. She'd want to read

a story about a brave boy who loved dogs more than anything.

"I guess I'm tired," he muttered, feeling his face get hot. "I just want to go to bed."

Aunt Rose looked sorry about everything, but she just said, "If that's what you want, then bed it shall be. Do you need any help? Would you like to have a bath?"

"No," Ben said. "I had a bath this morning."

"Go ahead, then. I'll come up later to look in on you."

Ben climbed the stairs with his back very straight. He turned on the light at the head of his bunk. He opened his bag and reached for his pajamas. There was something hard wrapped up in the bottoms. He undid it. It was a pocket-sized flashlight! Mum must have put it in so he wouldn't be scared at night. He swallowed, but the lump in his throat just got bigger.

He left the flashlight in the suitcase and put his pajamas on. Even though he had a light to read with, he didn't get out the book he had brought. He felt too miserable to read. He didn't even brush his teeth. He got under the covers and pulled them up to his chin. His hands were shaking. He reached up and switched off his light.

Nothing, not the bunk or the light or the supper, was nice anymore. He did not want to stay here. He wanted to go home. He wanted Mum and Dad. He even wanted Jimmy. Sunday afternoon seemed a hundred years away.

CHAPTER FOUR

The Mysterious Noises

Whack-whack-whack. Flip-flap. Thump-whack.

Ben Tucker opened his eyes. He stared up at the bunk above him. For a moment he could not figure out what it was. The light was coming from the wrong place, too. At home his bedroom window was right across from his bed. In this room he could tell it was in the wall at the foot of the bunk.

Bunk! He remembered in a flash. He was at Aunt Rose's house, and the first night of the weekend was over. Tomorrow his family would come. Ben smiled.

Flippity-flip. Whack-whack-whack!

Ben turned his head so that he could see what was making the strange noises. Then he froze.

Right next to his bed stood an enormous dog. A gigantic dog, a positive monster of a dog. Gully!

Ben gasped. He almost screamed, but he caught his breath in time. He must not let Gully know how scared he was. Dogs could smell your fear.

"They only attack people who are afraid of them," Jimmy had told him once. Ben stopped breathing. Maybe, if he did not move a muscle, Gully would go away.

Gully stayed right where he was. He was standing so close that Ben could have reached out and patted him. He had his mouth open so that he looked as if he were laughing. Ben did not think it was a friendly laugh. All he saw were Gully's big, sharp teeth. As Ben stared at him, Gully began to wag his tail. It thwacked against the bedside table.

Whack-whack-whack.

Then, as Ben still lay stiffly, holding his breath and praying Aunt Rose would come, the big dog shook himself. His ears flapped and his skin moved, somehow, as though it was too big for him, and his feet jigged a bit.

Flip-flap, thump, whackity-thump.

It was Gully who had made all the mysterious noises. Ben felt as though he was going to burst. He had to begin breathing again. He took the smallest breaths he could. He wanted to call Aunt Rose for help, but he was afraid to make a sound. He remembered a show he had seen on TV, where a policeman with a dog just Gully's size had cornered a bad guy.

"Make one false move," the policeman had said, "and Thor will tear you apart."

The man had reached for his gun anyway. Moving like a streak of lightning, the dog had flown at him and knocked him to the ground.

Ben shivered. He could still hear the man's scream.

Gully kept wagging his tail. That was a good sign. Had that police dog wagged his tail before he sprang? Ben couldn't remember.

Please, God, make him go away, he prayed silently.

Gully did not go. Instead he came even closer. Ben clutched at his sheet and opened his mouth to shriek. Before he could do it, though, a huge tongue had sloshed across his clenched hand. Ben was so astonished at the feel of it that he did not even squeak. Gulliver Gallivant's tongue was very soft, very wet and as big as a bath towel. It washed the back of Ben's hand thoroughly and then went on to lick his wrist and bare arm.

Maybe he's checking to see how I taste, Ben thought. Maybe any second now he'll take a big bite.

But he didn't believe it, not really. The big tongue was too gentle. It sort of tickled. Gully did not seem to notice his fear.

"Good boy," Ben said in a cracked whisper. "Good boy."

Gully's tail went twice as fast. It beat the bedside table as if it were a drum.

"Gully, where are you? Come and get it," Aunt Rose called from downstairs.

The large cream-coloured dog with the golden ears whirled around so fast that his paws skidded on the bare floor. He bounded out of the room without looking back once. Ben listened to him charging down the stairs. He did not slow down. He went full speed all the way to the bottom. He sounded like a whole stampede of dogs.

Very carefully, Ben slid out of bed. He tiptoed to the door and shut it tight. Then he went back to the bunk, sank down on it and shook.

"I hate dogs," he muttered. "I don't care if they're friendly or not. I don't like them and nobody can make me."

The back of his hand was still wet from Gully's tongue. Ben scrubbed it dry on the sheet. He'd have to use soap later to get the dog germs off.

He didn't know what he ought to do next. He wanted to crawl back into bed and go to sleep until his family came, but he knew Aunt Rose wouldn't let him. Besides, he was hungry.

He got up. He would get dressed right away while it was safe. He put on his clothes in such a hurry that he got his T-shirt on back to front and had to take it off and put it on again frontwards. He was glad nobody was there to see.

He was really hungry now. But where was that

awful dog? Ben went to the door and laid his ear against it. As he stood there, somebody knocked on the other side of the door. Ben jumped.

"Benjamin Tucker, are you up?" Aunt Rose's voice asked.

Ben opened the door. His aunt smiled down at him.

"Don't worry," she said, as if she knew all about the cold, scared feeling in the pit of his stomach. "Gully is outside. One of the neighbour children is playing with him. How did you like sleeping in my old room?"

"It was fine," Ben said politely.

"Would you like to take a look at your father's old room before breakfast?"

Ben nodded. He pushed his worry about Gully to the back of his mind. He really did want to see the room his father had slept in when he was a kid.

He followed Aunt Rose across the landing, up three steps and through a door to a wide hall with a tall double window at the far end. Ben realized that the tall window must be one of the big ones at the front of the house. He had never been in such a big house before. He stared at five more doors. The two open ones led to a bathroom and a little kitchen.

"How many rooms are there in this place?" he asked.

Dad had read *The Secret Garden* to him once. Misslethwaite Manor, in the book, had had over one hundred rooms. Their house in Vancouver had seven, eight if you counted the TV room in the basement.

Aunt Rose paused to think.

"Five bedrooms upstairs," she said. "Two small ones off the back hall and three larger ones in here. A small junk room that I've had converted into a kitchen. Two bathrooms, one front and one back. And downstairs there's my study, my kitchen, the dining room and the living room. Then there's a small bathroom down there plus my bedroom. How many is that?"

Ben wasn't sure, but he thought it had been fourteen. Wow! No wonder Dad liked this house so much. She hadn't counted the halls, either. The front hall was bigger than their living room in Vancouver.

Aunt Rose laughed at his look of astonishment.

"I know," she said. "It is far too big a place for one person to live in. But I've always loved large houses. And I'm going to rent this front part, don't forget. I've fixed up these two rooms on the left for your parents and Jimmy. Your father's old room was this front one."

Ben hurried to peer in. It was a big room with one of the wide double windows looking out onto the street. But it was disappointing. It was just like his parents' bedroom at home, not like a kid's room at all. Ben turned away.

"Here's where I'm putting Jimmy," Aunt Rose said.

Ben looked. It was an even larger room, newly painted and very empty except for one bed and a straight chair. "It's nice," Ben murmured. He wished there would be something interesting, something different. Misslethwaite Manor had been filled with neat old stuff.

They returned to the hall. There was one more closed door.

"Who slept in that one?" Ben asked, pointing.

"Our grandmother," Aunt Rose said. "I haven't finished painting it yet. Once your dad arrives, he can give me a hand. The ceilings are so high. Do you want to see it, too?"

Ben did. She went ahead of him again, talking as she went.

"Grandma was very strict about us never setting foot inside her door unless she had her eye on us. I still feel a bit strange coming in here without her permission, even though she died twenty years ago. Watch out for the ladder, Ben."

Ben dodged the stepladder which stood just inside the door. He stared around the empty room, trying to imagine Dad wanting to come into it when he was a kid. He couldn't. It didn't look one bit mysterious or interesting, just very bare.

"I'd better open the window and let some fresh air in here," Aunt Rose muttered. "I don't want your parents not to be able to sleep because of paint fumes."

While she was busy doing this, Ben went over to the closet and looked inside. It was just a very large closet, the kind you could walk into, with shelves going up one side and a rod for hanging up your clothes on the other. Then he glanced up.

Above his head, away up in the roof of the closet, there was a trap door!

Ben stood still and stared. He had always wanted to explore a house with trap doors and secret passages and locked rooms. No house he'd ever been inside had anything exciting like that. And now here, in his very own aunt's house, there was an actual trap door leading who knew where. He turned quickly to ask her about it.

Bang! Bang!

Aunt Rose was whamming the sash of the window to get it loose. Then she had to heave hard to raise it. By the time she had dusted her hands off on her jeans and turned to face him, he had changed his mind about asking.

The closet was still unpainted. Maybe nobody had noticed the trap door yet. Maybe, if Dad and

Aunt Rose hadn't been allowed in there, he was the only one who knew about it. No. Somebody had been in there after his great-grandmother had died because her things were gone. But whoever had cleared out the closet might never have looked up.

There was, at least, a chance that the trap door was his secret. This wasn't very likely, he knew, but it was possible. And if he was the only one who'd spotted it, as soon as he got time to himself, he'd find some way to get up there.

Ben shivered just thinking about it. But he was more excited than scared.

It might be dark up there, but he didn't mind the dark in the daytime. At least, he didn't think he did. And maybe it wasn't dark.

Maybe it led to an attic full of hidden treasures.

CHAPTER FIVE

Some Strange Girl

"You must be hungry, Ben," Aunt Rose said. "Let's get you some breakfast. We can go down the front way. I want to leave the front door open to help air the house. Go ahead and slide down the banister. Your father always did."

Ben swooped to the bottom while she was still just halfway down. It was great. He slithered off and followed her to the kitchen.

"This is your place," Aunt Rose said.

Ben slid into his chair and stared down at the writing on his placemat. The letters spelled BEN'S PLACE.

"Hey, it has my name on it," he said.

"So it does," Aunt Rose said. "I saw it in a store downtown one day. I thought it would make you feel at home."

She was nice. Jimmy was crazy. Ben smiled at her. Then he remembered how hungry he was. He stopped talking and drank his orange juice. It tasted just like the kind they had in Vancouver. Then he looked at the cereal. There were two brand-new unopened boxes.

Ben's face lit up. Both of them had prizes inside. Mum usually bought the large economy boxes without prizes. Jimmy and he ate a lot of cereal. Mum said the prizes were junk and Ben knew she was right, but he liked them, anyway.

Taking his time, he studied the pictures on each package. One was a kind of dart thing. It said it would shoot from three to four metres. The other was a little plastic spaceman. Ben chose the one with the dart in it. He could choose the other one tomorrow, if Aunt Rose didn't mind. He opened the box and peered inside. He couldn't see the dart. It must be buried under the cereal.

"Go ahead and dig for it," his aunt told him. "I bought them especially for you. Your hands are clean, aren't they?"

Ben started to nod. Then he remembered that he had not washed before he came down. And his right hand was covered with dog germs. He blushed.

"Never mind." Aunt Rose took down the hand towel hanging by the sink, wet it and handed it to him. "I didn't show you where your towels were last night, so it's as much my fault as yours. Give them a lick and a promise with this."

As he took the towel and scrubbed his hands hard, Ben wondered whether Aunt Rose knew about Gully's visit to his room. Was that why she said a *lick* and a promise? He didn't think so. He decided not to say anything about it. If he did, she might think he had made friends with Gully. He hadn't.

When he fished out the dart, it was very small, much smaller than the one in the picture. It looked as though it might break the first time you used it. And you had to have an elastic band to make it go. Aunt Rose got him one. Ben shot it the way the directions said. It only went a little way and then nose-dived to the floor. But it did work. It was better than nothing, whatever Mum said.

He poured the cereal into his bowl. Then he looked for the white sugar. He couldn't see any. Dad had said it was rude to ask for things that were not on the table. Ben tried brown sugar. He liked it.

When he had finished, he dried the dishes while his aunt washed. Once they were done, he asked if he could watch TV.

"I'm afraid not," Aunt Rose said. "I don't have a television."

Ben stared at her. No TV? Was she kidding? Everybody had a TV.

Aunt Rose chuckled.

"I know," she said. "You can't imagine life

without television. But when I decided to give up teaching, move back here, turn the upstairs into an apartment and try writing full time, I couldn't afford both a computer and a television. So no TV."

Well, at least she had a computer. That was something.

"You know, when I was your age, not everybody had a TV set. We didn't get one till I was eleven or twelve," Aunt Rose said.

Ben knew. Dad had told them, over and over, about not wasting his time on cartoons when he was a kid. Still, it was hard to picture.

"What did you do?" he said.

"Lots of things," his aunt said. "We put on plays. We built huts in the bush near our house. We went for hikes. We read a lot of books. Comic books, too. I found some of our old comics in a carton the other day and I put them in your room. They're in the big box beside the chest of drawers. But today is so lovely and sunny. It's a shame to stay inside. Why don't you go out in the backyard and play with Hana?"

"Who's Hana?"

"She lives next door," Aunt Rose said. "She's a couple of years older than you are, but she's the only child who lives at this end of the street. She's been asking and asking when you'd get here ever since I told her you were coming for a visit."

Ben did not want to play with some strange girl. He hated the way grown-ups tried to make you be friends with kids before you had a chance to find out what they were like. She sounded sappy, asking and asking when he'd get there. Yuck! Not only that, but if she was the only kid around, she must be the neighbour child who was playing with Gully. He definitely was not interested in playing with either girls or dogs. Besides, he had that trap door to think about. He did not meet his aunt's eyes.

"I think I'll go up and find those comics," he said. "I don't feel like playing outside right now."

As he headed for the stairs, though, he had to pass the kitchen window. He might as well take a quick look at this Hana. He paused and then came to a full stop.

The backyard was empty.

Where was Gully? The girl couldn't have taken him for a walk. With a small shiver Ben remembered how hard Gully had pulled on his leash the night before. No kid would be strong enough to hold onto him, if he decided to take off.

Then Ben saw the dog. He was in the yard after all. He came charging out from behind some bushes. He had a stick in his mouth. He ran in big leaping bounds. His caramel-coloured ears flew back. His tail waved joyously even while he was running. He held his head high in the air as if he wanted the whole world to see what a fine stick he had. Even Ben could see that he was having a wonderful time.

"Fetch, Gully. Bring it here," a voice called.

Then Ben saw the girl, too. She had been standing right up against the house, just to the right of the window. As she went to meet Gully, he got a good look at her.

She was bigger than he was. Her hair was long and straight and very black. It hung in bangs. She had on faded blue jeans. The T-shirt she wore had writing on it. As she stopped and turned sideways to him, Ben made out the words:

HANA UCHIDA
CHAMPION NUT

CHAPTER SIX

Hana Spills the Beans

Hana Uchida had a stick in her hand like the one Gully was fetching. She was waving it in the air and laughing.

Ben stayed at the window, watching. Gully raced up and slid to a stop right in front of Hana. He dropped his stick at her feet. Then he jumped up at her, trying to snatch the one she was still holding.

Ben shrank back. He expected to see her drop the stick and run for the house. She took a quick step backward instead.

"No, you don't, you big dope," Hana shouted at the excited dog. "Down! Down, I said!"

Ben's eyes stretched wide. He could not believe it when Gully backed up and went down on all his four feet. His pleading gaze went from the girl's face to the stick and back again. But he stayed down.

"Good boy!" Hana said, as though Gully had done something brilliant. "That's more like it. Okay. Fetch!"

The stick sailed all the way to the back fence. Gully tore after it. He moved so fast that he almost got there ahead of the stick. Hana laughed. Then she picked up the stick he had dropped at her feet and stood ready. Back came Gully, ears streaming out like banners.

Ben sucked in his breath. Would the dog leap up at her again? When Gully jumped, he went so high that his head was level with hers. He could knock her over as if she were a bowling pin. If he did knock her down, what would he do to her once she was on the ground?

Aunt Rose didn't seem worried. She was putting the clean dishes away, paying no attention to what was going on outside. Didn't she understand how dangerous dogs could be?

Gully did not knock Hana down. He dropped his stick neatly and just stood there, all his muscles bunched up, ready to chase the stick in her hand.

"Hana does love animals," Aunt Rose said from just behind Ben. She had come to watch the pair in the yard, after all. "She wants to be an animal trainer when she grows up. Most of the time, anyway. She does change her mind. It's a shame she can't have a pet of her own."

"Why can't she?" Ben asked, although he did not really care.

"Her parents think an animal would tie them down too much. They like to go skiing during the winter, and they travel quite a bit. Her father's family are still mostly in Japan, so they go there to visit every two or three years. Hana's very fond of her Japanese grandmother. But nothing makes up for not having a dog."

Hana had to be crazy, Ben thought.

Yet even though the game with the sticks did look frightening, it looked as though it might be sort of fun, too. Maybe he wouldn't mind throwing sticks for a dog if it was a very small dog and if he could be absolutely sure it would always drop the sticks nicely and never jump up or snap.

But you couldn't be absolutely sure of anything with dogs.

Now that dumb Gully was teasing Hana by bringing the stick to her, dropping it, and then grabbing it up before Hana could get it. Once he had it, he raced off in excited circles, looking back at the girl over his shoulder. Ben almost laughed. It was so plain that Gully wanted Hana to chase him and try to recapture the stick.

Aunt Rose did laugh.

"What a tease that dog is!" she murmured.

Hana pounced, doing her best to grab the stick.

Gully held on and growled at her. Ben heard the growl right through the window. He stiffened. Aunt Rose put her hand on his shoulder.

"He's only playing," she told him. "Don't worry. Hana knows how to handle him."

Ben did not say anything. He had forgotten all about the box of comics upstairs. He had even forgotten about the mysterious trap door. He leaned closer to the window.

Hana got hold of one end of the stick and pulled hard. Gully growled again. His tail was still wagging, but Ben did not notice. The second growl was louder than the first. It sounded ferocious. Ben could not believe his eyes when Hana let go of the stick and smacked the big dog across the nose with her open hand. Wasn't she afraid of anything?

"Bad boy! Cut that out," she scolded. "We are not playing Tug-of-war. We are playing Fetch. *Drop it!"*

Gully looked sad. But he had gotten the message. If he wanted to go on playing any game with Hana, he'd have to let her have the stick. It landed on her left sneaker.

"Ouch," Hana said, but not as though it really hurt. Then she added, "Good boy, Gully!"

Gully gave a small prance. But his eyes never left the stick. Finally it went winging through the air again. He dashed after it.

"Wouldn't you like a dog like that, Ben?" Aunt Rose asked softly. "You see now how playful and gentle he is."

The very idea shocked Ben. Everybody knew how he felt about dogs. Even Aunt Rose should have it straight by now. He opened his mouth to tell her exactly how much he hated dogs when Hana turned and spotted him at the window. Her face split in a broad grin. She waved.

"Hi!" she called. "Come on out and play with us."

Ben stared back at her. He shook his head. If only he had gotten away before she saw him!

"What's the matter? Are you sick?" she shouted, coming closer.

Ben felt trapped. He shook his head again and did his best to look unfriendly. The moment she turned away, he'd beat it up the back stairs to find those comic books.

Hana bent down and spoke to the dog.

"That's enough for now, Gully," Ben heard her say. "I have to go inside for awhile."

She was coming in. What if she brought that dog in with her?

"No, Gully," he heard her say then. "Miss Tucker told me to leave you outside. But I'll come back soon, I promise."

Then she was in the kitchen. She looked shy all

at once. Ben felt shy, too. He tried to think of a good reason for not going back out with her.

"Ben, this is my next-door neighbour, Hanako Uchida, known around here as Hana," Aunt Rose said. "Hana, you are so good with Gully. Tell Ben how gentle he is. He won't believe me."

"Gully is the most wonderful dog I know," Hana said. "He is so smart. He understands every word I say. Don't you think he's fantastic, Ben?"

Ben looked away from her. He felt dumb. It was his business how he felt about dogs, not Aunt Rose's or this girl's.

"He's okay, I guess," he mumbled, glaring at a little cactus plant on the shelf by the sink. "I don't like dogs much."

Hana stared at him as though he had suddenly grown two heads.

"You don't like dogs?" she gasped. "How can you not like dogs? Dogs are my favourite animal. Anyway, you'll have to get to like Gully, won't you? He's going to be your birthday present. Boy, are you lucky!"

CHAPTER SEVEN

Thunderstorm

Ben stared at Hana. What was she talking about? Gully was not his birthday present. His birthday was not until September. And, anyway, Gully was Bob's dog.

"You're crazy," he said at last. "Gully's not my dog. And it isn't my birthday."

But Hana was not looking at him. She was looking at Aunt Rose. And her face had turned crimson.

"Oh, Miss Tucker," she wailed, "I'm sorry. I didn't mean to tell. It just popped out. I forgot all about it being a secret."

Aunt Rose sighed and shook her head. She looked from Hana's worried face to Ben's puzzled one. She laughed suddenly. Then she pulled out a chair and sank down on it.

"It's all right, Hana," she said. "Poor Ben. He doesn't know what we're talking about. I'd better explain."

Ben waited. But she took a minute to get started.

"Gully is Bob's dog," she said. "But Bob and his wife have to move to England and they can't take Gully with them. They would have to leave the poor dog in quarantine for six months, and that wouldn't be fair to him. So Bob and his wife are looking for a new home for Gully. And I thought of you and Jimmy, especially you."

Ben stared at her. His mouth opened but no words came out. Aunt Rose went on quickly.

"Oh, I knew you weren't crazy about dogs. I called your father and asked him if I could give Gully to you for your birthday. He told me that they would like you to have a dog and that Jimmy has wanted one for ages. But he said that you were frightened of them. No dog, he said."

Now Hana was staring at Aunt Rose, too.

"You didn't tell me he said no," she whispered.

"Well, no, I guess I didn't," Aunt Rose admitted. "You see, I couldn't believe anyone could stay scared of Gully. I thought I'd invite him and Ben here together and, once they got to know each other, everything would be different."

Hana turned and looked straight at Ben, her brown eyes searching.

"Are you scared of dogs?" she demanded.

Ben looked down at his feet. He felt his cheeks grow hot.

"No, I'm not scared of dogs," he lied. "I just

don't like them. I don't want one, that's for sure!"

"You really don't want a dog?" Hana said. "You don't want Gully?"

Ben raised his head and glared back at her. Why didn't she mind her own business? He could hate dogs if he felt like it.

"I hate dogs," he flung at her. "They're vicious. They can even kill people. I saw it in the paper, so there!"

Hana tossed her head.

"We're talking about Gully," she said. "Gully isn't vicious, for Pete's sake. Gully wouldn't hurt a fly. People sometimes kill people, too. Does that make you scared of me? I'm a person. Boy, are you dumb!"

"I am not!" Ben yelled. He was so mad that he was afraid he might cry. He wanted to punch her as hard as he could.

"Okay, okay, cool down, both of you," Aunt Rose told them. "Just because you and I are nuts about dogs, Hana, doesn't mean Ben has to be, too. As for you, Ben, take it easy. Hana would love to have a dog like Gully. So it's hard for her to understand how you can pass him up."

She paused for breath. Neither Hana nor Ben spoke. Aunt Rose got up.

"Why don't we all have some oatmeal cookies and milk?" she suggested.

The two children still said nothing, but Ben stopped wanting to kick Hana. Although he had just finished breakfast, he was surprised to find he was starving. Maybe being mad made you hungry.

Aunt Rose got out the milk. Hana silently went to a cupboard and fetched the cookie tin. Then, as they started munching, Ben's aunt walked to the window and looked out. It was only then that Ben noticed that the room had grown much darker.

"Goodness, just look at that sky!" his aunt said. "I think we're in for a storm. Only an hour ago it was a lovely day. Now there's a real gale blowing."

Ben and Hana looked out the window. Ben was shocked to see great, purplish clouds piling up over half the sky. The tree branches were whipping back and forth. He could hear the wind. Then there was a sudden rumble of thunder, followed by a faint flicker of lightning.

Ben stiffened, clenching his hands until his knuckles went white. The other two didn't notice.

"I'll let poor Gully in," Hana cried, running to the back door.

"Wait a second, Hana," Aunt Rose called after her. "Ben, if you don't want to face Gully, you'd better go up to your room and shut the door."

Ben headed for the back stairs without a word. As he ran, he heard Aunt Rose begin to bang down windows. Then he heard Hana yell. She sounded scared.

"Miss Tucker, Gully's not in the yard," she was shrieking. "The gate's open and he's gone! I shut it when I came over. I'm positive I did!"

"I'm sure you did. It's blown open before, once or twice, when a gust of wind has caught it," Aunt Rose said hurriedly. "I forgot all about that when I told you to leave him out there."

"Oh, poor Gully!" Hana moaned.

"He's probably having the time of his life," Ben's aunt said, but her voice was worried. "Still, we'd better find him before he gets too far. I hope the rain holds off. He'll maybe go home, but there's nobody there to let him in. You look up the street in the other direction, Hana, and I'll go toward Bob's."

The back door slammed behind them. Ben heard them calling, "Here, Gully. Here, Gully." Then a spatter of rain drowned out their cries. Thunder growled again. It was closer this time.

Ben forgot all about Gully. He tore up the stairs to his room. He threw himself down on the bunk and buried his face in his pillow.

He was scared of the dark. He was scared of dogs. But he was terrified of thunderstorms. Lightning struck people dead all the time. It hit houses and killed people who thought they were safe inside. His parents said storms were beautiful and even Jimmy thought they were neat, but Ben hated them.

Suddenly he wondered if his window was still open. He lifted his head and took a quick look. It was! He could not make himself go over and shut it. The lightning might get him while he stood there.

Rumble. Bam!

Louder thunder! The open window was far too close.

Crash! He couldn't bear it.

Ben rolled over the edge of the bunk and scrambled underneath. It was dark there, and it smelled dusty. He rested his head on his arms. He was breathing fast. But the lightning would never come after him there.

Then, as his thudding heart quieted a little, he heard something totally unexpected. He heard a low whimper. He was not alone in his hiding place.

Gully was under there, too.

CHAPTER EIGHT

The Boy Who Hated Dogs

When Ben discovered that Gully was under the bed, he gave such a jump that he cracked his head hard on its sharp edge. Gully was pressed into the corner at the head of the bunk, but Ben could still have stretched out his hand and touched him. Gully was so close that Ben could hear every whimpering breath he drew.

He'd have to get out of there before Gully realized he had company. Maybe he could make it to the closet. He started to wriggle forward.

Bam! Crash! Crrrackle-BOOM!

Ben backed up so fast that he whacked his head again. The storm sounded as though it were right in the room with them. Thunder was still rattling the window when a blinding pink glare of lightning flashed across everything Ben could see. He gasped and covered his face with his arm. He couldn't make himself go out there, Gully or no Gully. Not with the window wide open.

Rumble-grumble-BAM!

Ben was shivering now and fighting not to cry. He did his best to keep still so that Gully wouldn't notice him. He could not figure out why Gully had hidden under the bed in the first place.

Then, all at once, he guessed. Wasn't Gully shivering even harder than he was? Hadn't he himself heard the big dog whimper? As the lightning flashed next time, he watched the dog. He was sure he saw Gully cover his eyes with one of his giant paws.

Gulliver Gallivant was as scared of thunderstorms as Ben Tucker.

He's too big to be afraid, Ben thought. Then he remembered Dad saying, "You're too big to be such a crybaby, Ben." Being big did not help a bit.

The thunder roared again. Gully moaned.

"It's okay, Gully," Ben found himself saying. He did his best to sound like Dad. "Lightning usually just jumps from cloud to cloud. It hardly ever strikes things down here. By the time we see it flash, it's already struck, really."

Gully stayed scrunched down. There wasn't room to do anything else. But when Ben spoke to him, his tail gave a feeble thunk against the floorboards. And, the next moment, he began to creep toward Ben. The boy hesitated, and then kept talking.

"You can even tell how far away the storm is. If you can count in between the lightning and the thunder, then it isn't too close. You have to count like this. One-thousand-and-one. One-thousand-and-two."

Ben was amazed. He sounded just like a grown-up. He went on, not really sure whether he was talking to Gully or himself. Although Gully was touching him now, he did not shift his position.

"This is only sheet lightning, too. At least, I think it is. My father says sheet lightning never hurt . . ."

This time the flash of lightning came right on top of the crack of thunder. Without stopping to think, Ben clutched at Gully. His face went down onto Gully's warm fur and his arm wrapped itself around the dog's great neck. He did not remember that this was a dog and he was afraid of dogs. He just held on tight and waited for the lightning to strike them both.

Gully turned his head and gave Ben's ear a quick lick. Then they both waited.

The next peal of thunder was not quite so loud. Ben raised his head a little and listened. Could it be true? Was the worst part over already? It was. The storm, which had blown up so fast, was leaving as quickly as it had come.

Carefully, Ben loosened his grip on Gully's neck. Had he really been hugging a dog? He wriggled backwards a bit.

But Gully was still shaking. He did not understand that the storm was going away. His brown eyes met Ben's. Then the big Lab dropped his head onto his paws and gave a long sigh that ended in a little whimper.

"It's okay, Gully," Ben heard himself saying again. He stopped backing away. Gully's tail thunked once. Ben drew a deep breath. He reached out his hand and stroked the broad head.

"It's over, boy," he said. "It's all over."

Gully's tail whacked the floor twice, real wags now. Ben laughed. It was a shaky laugh but who cared? Nobody heard him but Gully. He tried scratching behind the velvety ear closest to him. Dogs were supposed to like that. Gully stopped trembling. He moved his head so that Ben's fingers would hit exactly the right spot. He grunted.

Ben laughed and scratched harder.

"Hey," he said softly, "you're not such a dragon, after all. You're a big marshmallow."

Then he heard a door downstairs bang shut.

"I couldn't find him," Ben heard his aunt say. "I'll call the animal shelter. He's only been gone

HANA UCHIDA
CHAMPION
NUT

for ten minutes, but maybe somebody has seen him."

"Hey, Miss Tucker, look! The front door's been open all along," Hana said. "Maybe he came into the house again!"

Ben did not wait for them to come up and catch him hiding under the bed. He slithered out, making as little noise as possible.

"Come on out, boy," he said softly over his shoulder. "They think you're lost. Do you want them to know you're a chicken?"

Gully stirred but stayed put. He could still hear the thunder, even if Ben couldn't.

Ben went to the door.

"Aunt Rose, I've found Gully," he called. "He's up here under my bed."

Had she heard him? Maybe he should go down. But he did not really want to leave Gully. Ben knew how much he hated being left alone when he was scared. If only he could coax the dog out from under the bed. If he sat down on the floor and talked to him, what would happen?

He might come leaping out. The thought of Gully back on all four feet made Ben stop to think. Gully quivering with fear was one thing. Gully wild and on the loose was quite another. Instead of getting down on the floor, he pulled a chair over to the bunk.

The next minute, Aunt Rose and Hana came running up the stairs. But when they reached the bedroom door, they stopped and just stood there, staring.

There sat Ben Tucker, the boy who hated dogs. On his feet rested the head of Gulliver Gallivant. And Ben was leaning down, scratching behind one of Gully's floppy ears.

CHAPTER NINE

Ben Takes Command

When Hana and Aunt Rose stopped in their tracks and stared, Ben could feel his face growing pink. He turned his head away from them. He gazed down at Gully, instead. Gully's tail banged the floor. The sound of it made Ben smile.

"Where did you find him, Ben?" Aunt Rose said then.

Ben wanted to hug her. She could have said, "How come you're sitting there patting Gully? Last night you wouldn't even stay in the same room with him." But she hadn't.

Hana did not give him time to answer. She was not tactful like Aunt Rose. She took a step forward and blurted, "How come you're patting him like that? I thought you were scared of dogs. You said they were vicious!"

Ben scowled at her.

"I did not say I was scared of dogs. I said I didn't like them and I don't want one for a present. That's all I said."

He turned from her. He spoke to Aunt Rose.

"I think he must have gone out the gate and then heard thunder and run in through the front door," he said. "I found him hiding under the bed. He was away back in the corner, shivering and crying."

Hana dropped to her knees and flung her arms around Gully's neck. She rubbed her cheek on the top of his head. Her hair was wet with rain.

"Poor Gully," she crooned. "I wish I'd known. I'd have comforted you."

"That must have been what happened," Ben's aunt said. "I remember Bob saying that Gully's been afraid of storms ever since he was a puppy. It seems so silly in such a big dog."

Aunt Rose was just like Dad. If Gully were a boy, she'd say, "You're too big to be such a crybaby, Gully."

Gully had lifted his head off Ben's feet. He was busy licking Hana's face and right ear. He had wriggled forward and was now half out from under the bed. He did not look frightened any longer. Soon he'd be all the way out and back on his feet. Ben stood up and started to shift the chair.

Instantly the big dog scrambled out and gave a

mighty shake. Ben jumped away in spite of himself. Gully lying down, whimpering with fright, he could take. This Gully, so much taller, his mouth wide open so that his big teeth showed, all ready to romp and knock people over, he wanted no part of.

"You are so scared of him!" Hana cried, getting up, too. "I knew it. What a baby!"

Before Ben had a chance to answer back, she burst into giggles.

"Boy, it would have been a scream if you'd been scared of lightning, too, and hidden under the bed and then Gully had come running and crawled under there with you. I bet you'd have died on the spot!"

"Stop teasing him, Hana," Aunt Rose said. "It's a good thing he was here to comfort Gully since you and I weren't. I think that was very brave, Ben."

Hana stopped laughing and looked ashamed.

"That's right," she said, giving Gully another hug. "It's a good thing Ben wasn't scared. Right, boy?"

Gully looked at Ben. Ben looked at Gully. Ben had a feeling that even if Gully could have told on him, he wouldn't have. He smiled at the dog. He watched the long whip of a tail wag in response. If only the dog were not so big and rough, he might be okay.

"Hana," Aunt Rose asked, starting to leave the room, "can you stay for lunch?'

"No, I can't," Hana said. She looked worried all at once. "What time is it? I have to be home at ten to take my cousin to the library. It isn't past ten, is it?"

"You have exactly eleven minutes," Ben's aunt said. "Maybe Ben would like to go, too."

"No, he wouldn't," Hana said, before Ben had a chance to answer. "My cousin is four and he's a real pain. Mum has to stay home and babysit him all afternoon so I said I'd give her a break. It's a special story hour for pre-schoolers."

"I want to look at those comics," Ben said.

"I'll come over right after lunch," Hana told him. "See you then."

So who asked you? Ben wanted to say. But he kept quiet.

She ran off down the stairs. Aunt Rose paused and looked at the boy and the dog. Gully had not dashed off after Hana. He was standing looking at Ben and wagging his tail.

"I have to get us some lunch and make some sandwiches I've promised to send to the church this afternoon," Aunt Rose said. Then she went on in a soft voice. "Gully certainly seems to like you, Ben, even if you don't like him much. Shall I take him downstairs or may he stay with you?"

Ben opened his mouth to say she should take him. But before he got a word out, Gully lay down again by the chair and put his head back on his paws. Then he rolled his eyes up so he could look at Ben. His tail thumped the floor twice.

Ben did not want to be left alone with a dog. But Gully was trying so hard to be good.

"I . . . I guess he can stay here," Ben said slowly.

Aunt Rose did not wait for him to change his mind. She left almost as swiftly as Hana had done. Ben and Gully were on their own.

Ben sat down quickly and didn't move for a full minute. Gully lay and watched him. He didn't look dangerous. But Ben did not trust him. He remembered the way the dog had leaped up at Hana, trying to snatch the stick from her hand.

At last he had to do something. He half turned in the chair, searching for the box of old comics. It was right beside the dresser, just out of reach. He would have to stand up and lean way forward to get his hand into it. Could he do that without disturbing the dog?

It took him a long minute to get up enough nerve. Then he stood up slowly and carefully.

At once Gully was on his feet. Ben froze. Gully waited for something to happen. Ben sat down again. Gully looked disappointed. But he sat down, too, still watching Ben.

Then Ben remembered Bob giving the dog orders. Hana had, too. The boy took a deep breath.

"Gully, lie down," he said.

He meant to speak firmly, but his voice squeaked and wobbled. Gully put his head on one side and seemed puzzled. Ben gulped and tried again. This time his voice came out in almost a shout. As he gave the command, he pointed at the floor, the way Bob had done the night before.

"Gully, *lie down!*"

To the boy's amazement, the big dog sank to the floor. He, Ben Tucker, had made this enormous dragon of a dog lie down. He could hardly believe it.

He looked at the dog stretched out at his feet.

"Stay, Gully," he said and stood up.

Gully looked mournful, but he did not get up. Ben didn't want to step over the dog to reach the comics. But he did manage to pull the box toward him until it was close enough for him to be able to reach in. There was a big pile of comics, a beat-up tennis ball and a dented mouth organ in the box. Ben quickly grabbed the top three comics and sat down.

He felt as if he had been running very fast.

Yet Gully, although he had watched Ben with interest, had not moved. It was wonderful.

Then Ben remembered the way Bob and Hana had praised the dog when he did what he was told.

He leaned forward and ran his fingers lightly over Gully's broad head.

"Good boy," he said softly.

Whack, went the tail.

The comics were neat. Ben began to read about Captain Marvel. After a couple of pages he stole a look at the dog.

Gulliver Gallivant was sound asleep.

CHAPTER TEN

The Trap Door

Ben read two more comic books before he got bored. Gully was still asleep. Ben looked at his watch. It was ten minutes past eleven. He had lots of time to do something else before lunch.

The trap door! How could he have forgotten about it?

Ben studied the sleeping Lab. He looked so peaceful. Could he get away without disturbing him?

Keeping his eyes fixed on the dog, Ben eased himself up off the chair. Gully went on sleeping. He had rolled onto his side and was sprawled full length, snoring gently. He did not flicker an eye-lash.

Ben took a deep breath and stepped over Gully's hind legs. Gully snored on. Moving with great care, Ben crept forward one step at a time. Gully did not move.

Six seconds later Ben was out the door and

crossing the hall to go up to the front of the house. He still moved on tiptoe. He was not sure Aunt Rose would like him exploring in her house without permission. But he didn't want to tell her. This was his private adventure. He wanted the trap door, and whatever lay above it, to be his secret.

He had to open the door to the apartment part of the house. As he reached for the doorknob, he listened hard. Aunt Rose chose that moment to turn on the radio down in the kitchen. Music poured up the stairs. Ben grinned. She'd never hear now. She might not stay in the kitchen, though. He'd still have to be careful. He turned the knob slowly until he heard the latch click open. The click sounded terribly loud.

He waited a moment, holding his breath. Neither Gully nor Aunt Rose came to investigate. He shut the door behind him but did not pull it tight. He didn't want any more loud clicks.

The wide hall stretched ahead of him. All he had to do now was walk to the front bedroom on the right. If only his steps didn't make the floorboards creak so much!

He was there. He closed the bedroom door behind him. Then at last he went into the closet and peered up at the small, square trap door in the ceiling, far above his head.

It was awfully high up, over twice his height.

They sure built tall rooms in the olden days. If it weren't for the ladder, he would have no hope of reaching it. But there stood the ladder in the bedroom, ready and waiting.

It was a stepladder made of metal. It was much taller than he was. It was too heavy for him to carry, but he thought he might be able to push it across the floor. He tried shoving it a little. It shifted easily but it clanked and rattled. Well, the doors were shut. He'd have to take a chance.

Bit by bit, holding his breath and listening hard in case Aunt Rose called to ask what he was doing, Ben pushed the ladder across to the closet door. There he had to stop. The ladder, with its legs spread out, was too wide to go through the door.

Ben paused to think things over. If he turned the ladder and put it in step side first, it might work.

He had quite a struggle turning the ladder. Once it almost toppled over on top of him. Then, as the top of the ladder neared the door frame, Ben tensed. Was it going to slide under, or was it going to stick?

It just barely slid under. Perfect.

Ben checked to see that the ladder was placed right under the trap door. When he had it exactly the way he wanted it, he sat down on the bottom step for a moment to catch his breath. Sitting there, he tipped his head back and stared up at the distant opening. What would he really find up there?

Skeletons. That's what Jimmy would have told him.

But Ben wasn't scared. Not scared enough to give up, anyway. Besides, there wouldn't be anything too terrible in his own great-grandma's attic.

Then he remembered that other people had lived here after she died. Strangers had rented the house while Aunt Rose was living in Hearst. Maybe they had killed somebody and hidden the body up in this attic.

Ben forced a laugh. What a crazy idea. He'd never show Jimmy and Hana and Dad he wasn't a baby unless he got moving.

He stood up and squared his shoulders. He began to climb. When he got halfway up, he could feel his knees starting to shake. It looked so far down to the floor. But he did not stop. He just went more slowly. When he got to the second step from the top, he thought he could reach the ceiling. But first he'd have to let go of the ladder with both hands and straighten up to his full height. Could he?

It would help a lot if the ladder didn't keep trembling. Or did it only shake because he did?

He thought of Jimmy, of Hana saying, "What a baby!"

Very, very slowly, he straightened up to his full height. He felt dizzy. He had nothing to hold onto, only the flat wall. No, there were the shelves on his left, going almost all the way up. But if he reached over to them, he might lose his balance.

Biting his lips and bracing his knees against the very top of the ladder, Ben reached up his hands as high as they would go. His fingertips brushed something solid. He was touching the trap door!

He was so excited that he leaned back to look up, and wobbled wildly. He waved his arms for a moment, and then caught his balance again. He stayed very still and breathed slowly to steady himself. He counted to five. Then he reached up again.

He pushed at the wood with his fingertips. It didn't budge. He pushed harder with his whole hands. Suddenly, he felt it give a tiny bit. He was going to be able to open it. He shoved again, harder. He saw a crack open around the edge of the trap door and darkness beyond.

Then, below him, the bedroom door swung open. Gulliver Gallivant came padding into the room.

"Oh, no!" Ben gasped, staring down at the dog and swaying dangerously on the ladder.

Gully looked up and spotted him. His tail began to wag. He came over to the foot of the ladder and nosed around it.

At the same moment, Ben heard Aunt Rose.

"Benjamin Tucker," she called, "lunch is ready."

CHAPTER ELEVEN

What to Do with Gully

Ben wanted to cry. Here he was at the top of a wobbly ladder. He had just gotten the trap door to move. And now Aunt Rose wanted him to come to lunch and Gully was at the foot of the ladder!

He couldn't climb down, not with that dog cutting off his way to the door. Soon Aunt Rose would come and find him. She would ask questions, and everything would be spoiled. His adventure was over before it had started.

But it wasn't. Not yet, anyway.

Gully had heard Aunt Rose calling, too. At the sound of her voice, his ears perked up. Then he spun around and went racing toward the kitchen.

The instant the dog was out of sight, Ben reached down and got hold of the top of the stepladder. Then he climbed shakily down. He ran after the dog, going lightly so that Aunt Rose would not know where he was coming from. When he got downstairs, he found his aunt spoiling Gully with a dog biscuit.

"Hi," she said, smiling at him. "Those old comic books must have been spellbinding. I haven't heard a peep out of you for hours."

Ben smiled back, but he did not look her straight in the eye.

"They were great. I've never seen such old ones before." He bit into his hamburger hungrily. Gully sat beside him and watched every bite going up to his mouth.

"You and Gully seem to have made friends," Aunt Rose said, handing him a bowl of salad.

"Mmmm. This is good!" Ben said, taking an especially large bite and chewing noisily. He didn't want to talk about himself and Gully.

Aunt Rose grinned at him and changed the subject. They talked about their favourite books. Ben loved *The Minerva Program*. Aunt Rose liked it, too. She said she couldn't choose just one favourite, though. She liked so many.

Then the phone rang. When Aunt Rose came back to the table, she looked worried.

"Ben, I'm afraid I have to go out this afternoon. Remember my telling you I had to make sandwiches? A member of our church died on Thursday and a group of us are providing refreshments for the family after the funeral. That call was from my friend Rhondda. Another woman who was supposed to help has sprained her ankle and Rhondda just found out. So they need somebody to take her place. I'm really sorry, because I wanted to spend the afternoon with you. But I can't let Rhondda down. She was going to pick up the sandwiches because my car is being repaired. So I told her she could pick me up, too."

Ben tried to make sense out of all this. Did it mean *he* was going to have to spend Saturday afternoon in church? Or would she let him stay home by himself? If she would, he'd be able to explore without worrying about getting caught.

But Aunt Rose hadn't finished.

"I know! I'll call Meg Uchida." Her look of worry disappeared. "Hana said she'd come over here, but instead you can spend the afternoon over there helping them to babysit her little cousin."

"I'd be okay here by myself," Ben said, trying not to sound too eager.

"I'm sure you would," his aunt said. "But I can't leave you here all alone."

"I'd have Gully," Ben said, to his own astonishment.

Aunt Rose laughed at him. She reached out and stroked Gully's soft ears.

"I'll let him out before I leave," she said. "When

you go to the Uchidas', he can just stay here. Gully's used to spending time alone."

She stood up as if everything was settled, and got Ben a large bowl of strawberries and ice cream. Then she went to call Mrs. Uchida.

As Ben started on his dessert, he could hear her dial the number over and over.

"Meg is hopeless," she muttered, after trying the number for the sixth time. "I don't know what she finds to talk about. I'd better get into some decent clothes and try her again when I'm ready."

She vanished. Ben stirred his ice cream to make it soft. He loved it that way but Mum said it wasn't polite. Aunt Rose came back just as he finished the last spoonful. She let Gully out and then back in and returned to the phone.

Before she had time to dial, a car horn honked. Aunt Rose went to the front door, waved to her friend, ran back and snatched up a piece of paper. She scribbled a note on it and shoved it across the table at Ben.

"I can't get through to Meg and Rhondda's waiting," she said, grabbing up the tray of sandwiches. "The note explains everything. Take it next door as soon as you finish. Just pull the back door shut behind you. It'll lock itself. I know Meg won't mind having you. She'll be in all afternoon. I was talking to her this morning after Hana left. I'll be home around four o'clock, but if you're having fun, don't hurry back. I must fly!"

The next moment, the front door banged. She was gone. And he had the house all to himself.

Ben felt like singing. Mrs. Uchida didn't know he was supposed to be coming over so she'd never miss him. And he could get up to that trap door while Aunt Rose was out.

He made himself sit still and count to one hundred slowly just to be sure. Then he sprang up and ran to his room. Gully was at his heels, but he was too excited to care. He got his flashlight. Boy, would Mum ever have a fit if she knew how he was using it!

He went up to the room where the trap door was. Then he realized that he had to do something with Gully. What if the dog knocked over the ladder? Ben stared down at him, thinking hard. He didn't dare try to push him through the door leading out of the apartment. Gully might snap.

He went ahead of him instead, calling, "Come on, boy. You'll like it better out here."

Gully followed him eagerly. But the moment Ben turned to go back through the door, Gully wheeled about, too, and went ahead of him.

"No, Gully," Ben begged. "You stay out there."

He pointed. Gully looked to see what he was pointing at. Then he gazed up at Ben with puzzled eyes.

Ben had an inspiration. In the box of comic books, there was that old tennis ball. If he got the ball and threw it down the stairs, Gully would chase after it and he could shut the door on him before he got back.

He raced to his room and found the ball. The minute Gully spotted it, his eyes lit up and his tail wagged furiously. Ben felt uneasy. What if the dog leaped for it? He hurried back to the head of the stairs before Gully had a chance to think of trying any tricks and threw the ball all the way to the bottom.

It worked. Gully almost turned a somersault in his dash down after it.

But before Ben could get behind the door to the apartment, the dog had come flying back. He dropped the ball right at Ben's feet. He was so happy and excited that Ben had to pick it up and throw it a few more times.

It was a good idea, anyway. He would tire the dog out. Then Gully would fall asleep again and Ben would have his chance.

Away went the ball. Away went the dog, tumbling downstairs, galloping up again with it in his mouth. Soon the tennis ball was wet with spit. Ben picked it up gingerly. But Gully wouldn't let him give up quite yet.

The game grew so lively that Ben almost forgot

the trap door. Then he noticed that Gully was getting out of breath. Good. Now if he could just get him to lie down . . .

"Hi, Ben," called Hana's voice from the kitchen. "Hi, Gully. I'm back."

CHAPTER TWELVE

Hana Is Scared

When he heard Hana call, Ben was so mad that he wanted to kick somebody. No, not just somebody. Hana Uchida. Who did she think she was, marching into his aunt's house as if she owned it? Who had asked her to come? Nobody. Who wanted her? Nobody. She'd wreck everything.

He'd have to get rid of her.

Maybe, if he just didn't answer, she'd give up and go away. He didn't think Hana was the kind of girl who gave up easily, but he stayed absolutely still and hoped.

Hana came into the downstairs hall. He watched her over the banister. She hadn't seen him.

Then Gully, impatient at the delay in their game, gave a small whimper of protest. Hana looked up. Ben did not smile. Her eyes widened in surprise. Maybe she'd gotten the message. But it wasn't Ben's scowl that had startled Hana.

"Hey, how come you're playing with Gully?" she demanded.

She was not pleased. Maybe she didn't want Gully to be friends with anybody but her. Ben wondered why the dog hadn't rushed down to greet her. Then he saw the reason. Gully's brown eyes had never left the ball. He was still waiting for the game to go on.

As if he played with dogs every day, Ben tossed the ball down the stairs. Gully flew after it.

"I guess I can play with him if I like," Ben said. "You were the one who said I was scared of him, not me."

Hana tossed her head. Her eyes flashed.

"If you weren't scared of him, why did Miss Tucker ask me to keep him outside so you, poor little sucky baby, could have your breakfast in peace. I guess Miss Tucker doesn't tell lies. Besides, your own father said . . ."

Ben swung around and glared down at her. He could feel his face burning.

"You leave my dad out of this," he bellowed. "I never said Aunt Rose told lies. She made a mistake, that's all. Just because I didn't want a dog around when I was eating doesn't mean I'm scared of them. And I am not a sucky baby. I bet you wouldn't have nerve enough to do what I'm going to do in a minute, so there."

At once, Hana's dark eyes gleamed with interest. She came up the stairs almost as fast as Gully.

"What are you going to do? Tell me. I'll bet it's nothing much. Whatever it is won't scare me, that's for sure."

Ben was mad at himself now. Why had he gone and said such a dumb thing? There must be some way to get out of telling her. If she'd just give him time to think, he'd come up with something.

But she didn't give him time. Instead she burst out laughing as he hesitated.

"I knew it!" she crowed. "You can't think of one thing to say, can you? What a baby! Bragging about nothing."

"Follow me," Ben growled and led the way through the apartment door. She followed him without a word. So did Gully. Once they were inside the front bedroom, Ben grabbed her arm and jerked her forward to the foot of the ladder. Then he pointed up to the trap door, high above them.

"See that trap door? I'm climbing up to find out what's up there."

Hana's eyes widened. She pulled her arm free and backed up a step.

"You can't go up there. Miss Tucker won't let you."

Ben couldn't believe it. Hana sounded nervous.

"Aunt Rose has gone out," he said. "I'll be up and down again before she gets home. She won't be back till around four o'clock."

Hana bit her lip and looked at him sideways. Ben felt great.

"The ladder doesn't go high enough," she said.

She was scared. She really was. Who was the baby now? Not Ben Tucker.

"You can come, too," he said, keeping his face straight. Then, looking her in the eye, he added softly, "Or are you too chicken?"

She looked so terrified that he almost burst out laughing. He couldn't believe he had beaten her this easily. What was the matter with her?

Wait a minute. He didn't really want her to climb up there with him, did he?

Suddenly, he knew that he did. It would be more fun with two. He'd have to talk fast, though, to persuade her. She wasn't even pretending now not to be scared. Yet this was the girl who had whacked Gully across the nose when he wouldn't give her the stick.

"The ladder goes a long way up," he told her. "You can reach the edge of the trap door from there and get a grip on it with your hands. I already tried that before lunch so I know. You're bigger than I am. It should be even easier for you. Once we get that far, then we can go up the last bit by swinging our feet over and using the shelves. See?"

He pointed to the shelves that went up the side of the closet. Hana barely glanced at them.

"They don't look all that strong," she objected. She added more loudly, "They don't go all the way to the top, either."

"They do, too. Use your eyes," Ben told her. "And they're plenty strong enough. My great grandmother used them to put heavy things on for years and years. Would I trust them if they weren't safe? No way. Any other excuses?"

"It's awfully dark up there!"

He fished his flashlight out of his pocket and shone it up so she could see how bright it made things. But she still didn't look convinced.

"My mum would be mad," she said. "It doesn't look safe. I hate climbing up things. I'm not allowed to climb trees. My dad fell out of a tree when he was a kid and broke his arm in three places."

"So what?" Ben said. "This isn't a tree. Anyway, I knew all along that you wouldn't have the nerve. So go ahead and stay down here where you won't get hurt. I'm going up."

He dropped his flashlight back into his deepest pocket. He needed both hands free. He put one foot on the bottom rung of the ladder. Something bumped into it, making it jiggle. He glanced down.

It was Gully.

Ben took his foot off the ladder. What if Gully got all excited and jumped at the ladder and made it rock when he was at the top? Ben's stomach lurched at the very thought.

"Help me put Gully out of this part of the house," he said gruffly to Hana. "I don't know how to get him to leave."

"Boy, are you helpless!" she said, sounding like herself again. She took Gully by his collar. "Come on, Gulliver."

Gully trotted along happily. When they reached the door out of the apartment, Hana opened it and she and Gully walked through. She pointed at the floor and started to order Gully to lie down.

Then Ben saw her hesitate. Gully was gazing up at her as if his heart was breaking. Even Ben could tell that Gully did not want to be left out there all by himself. Hana looked up at Ben.

"I'll be back in a second," she said.

She ran down the stairs. Gully looked after her, went down a couple of steps, swerved and returned to Ben who was standing in the doorway. He was staring hard at Ben's pocket, the one bulged out by the tennis ball. Ben pretended not to understand.

What was Hana doing? Had she chickened out and gone home? He was surprised at how much he wanted her to come back.

Suddenly a blare of music made him jump. Then he heard a voice saying, "This is CJOY in Guelph, Ontario." Hana came running back, a wide smile on her face. When she reached the landing, she called Gully and made him lie down. Then she gave him a big cookie. While he crunched it, his tail thudding the carpet, she slipped through the door and closed it behind her.

"I put the radio on to keep him company," she said. "That's what my aunt does for her canary."

On the far side of the door, Gully whimpered.

"Be a good boy and stay, Gully," Hana called to him.

They both heard the dog give a great sigh. Then he flopped back down on the floor.

Ben had had enough of Gully. He spun around and marched back to the room that used to be his great-grandmother's. He was glad now that Hana was there. It *was* dark inside the closet. That morning the sun had been shining through the front window and it had been much brighter. But now the sun was on the other side of the house, and even the room outside the closet seemed shadowy.

Ben closed the bedroom door tightly this time. Then he went straight to the stepladder. Without giving himself a chance to think it over, he began to climb.

Hana stood at the bottom and stared up at him, her eyes wide. Somehow that made the climb easier.

He was at the top. He pushed the trap door. It moved. He managed to shift it a little. All he could see through the crack was darkness. He had his flashlight, though. Should he shine it through the crack before he tried swinging up?

"Oh, Ben," Hana quavered from the foot of the ladder, "I don't think you should go up there. What if Miss Tucker finds out? Or my mum? We'll be in big trouble."

Ben knew then that if he waited to get out his flashlight, he'd lose his nerve. He held onto the crack with both hands, swung his feet onto the first shelf, then the second. Then he freed one hand and gave the trap door the hardest shove he could. It banged up, showering his face with bits of dirt. And with a great scramble with his feet and hoist with his hands, Ben was through the trap door.

He sat on the edge, his heart pounding so hard he felt it might burst. Then he looked down between his knees at Hana's anxious face far beneath him.

"So who's a sucky baby now?" he said.

CHAPTER THIRTEEN

Trapped

Ben laughed down at Hana, but really he was scared. What would he see when he flashed the light around up here? It sure smelled queer and dusty.

"What's it like?" Hana was asking. "What do you see?"

He got out the light. His hands were not steady so he gripped it tightly. Suppose he dropped it? The very thought made him feel cold all over.

Click.

A streak of light sprang across the darkness, making Ben jump. He swung the light in a wide arc so that it swept the whole space. It was like a big empty cave up there. He was sitting on a beam that went right across the attic. The roof sloped down to the floor away out at the edges and met at a ridge pole far above him. Other beams crisscrossed the floor and in between them was a lot of brown matted stuff.

Ben stretched out his hand and touched some

of it. It was rough. It had prickly bits in it. He pulled his fingers back and rubbed them on his jeans. Insulation! That was what it was. They'd put some in their house in Vancouver to help keep the fuel bills down. He had felt it then and it had made his hand sting just like this.

He flashed the light into the far corners. No skeletons. No treasures, either. But it was a neat place. As his eyes got used to the darkness, he saw that there were gaps here and there around the edges. He could see bits of daylight through them. There was nothing to be scared of up here. And he had discovered this great place by himself.

Suddenly he remembered Hana. He peered down at her.

"Come on up," he urged. "It wasn't hard, honest. You won't fall. It's neat up here. Come on. Just try."

He could tell she was wavering. He kept talking.

"You can see for yourself that it's safe. If I can do it, you can. You're taller. It's really neat up here. You've got to see it."

"Is it . . . what's up there?" she asked.

Ben hardened his heart. The only way to get her up was to keep her curious. And to make her ashamed, too, of not being as brave as he was. It would be lots more fun with two of them. If she stayed down there, he'd have to go down, too, and the adventure would be over.

"Hurry up," he snapped at her. "You'll like it. I can't explain it. You have to see it for yourself. Don't be such a big suck."

She glowered at him. Good. If she got mad enough, she'd do it just to show him. He waited.

"I can help you with the last bit," he put in. "You can grab my hands and I'll haul you up."

Hana clutched each side of the ladder and started up. Her jaw was set. She was staring straight ahead and breathing hard. Then, as she got to the top, she glanced down. Ben heard her gasp. Then she seemed to freeze.

He couldn't think what to do. He could see the ladder beginning to shake. If he didn't figure out some way to help, she might lose her grip and fall.

He swung himself over on his stomach and reached down both hands.

"Grab hold," he yelled at her. "Come on!"

Hana snapped out of her trance. She ignored his outstretched hands. She gulped in a sobbing breath, grabbed the edge of the opening and began to swing up the way he had done.

Crack!

The shelf creaked under her weight and began to give. Hana screamed and sprang up to the top one. It came loose and crashed down on the one beneath. Before it went, she was up through the opening, half in, half out. Ben pulled at her with all his strength and she gave one final desperate wriggle. She was safe!

Ben was so terrified that he couldn't speak or move. Hana began to cry in noisy sobs.

"I knew we shouldn't," she wailed. "I told you it was dangerous. My mum will kill me when she finds out!"

Ben sat up. Where had the flashlight gone? He couldn't have let it fall, could he? No. It was right beside him. He picked it up and turned it on. He pointed the beam at Hana.

"Stop crying," he said. Then he heard himself add, "You're too big to be such a crybaby."

That made him laugh. It wasn't much of a laugh but he knew that it was better than crying.

"I'll go down," he told Hana, "and get help."

Hana clutched at him.

"No!" she shrieked. "Don't leave me alone up here. Besides, you'll fall and get killed."

Ben looked down at the shelves. The top one had landed on the second one, the one that had made that awful cracking sound. Hana must weigh a lot more than he did. They had felt perfectly safe to him. If he hung by his hands, his feet would reach the ladder. But suppose he couldn't find it? He was no good at gym. He knew he couldn't pull himself back up to safety if the ladder wasn't right there. It was a very long way to the floor.

"Okay," he said. "I'm not going anywhere. For Pete's sake, pipe down. There's nothing to worry about. Aunt Rose will be home soon. She'll get us down."

Hana's sobs grew a little quieter. Soon they were more like sniffles.

"I thought you said she wouldn't be home till after four o'clock," she muttered. "I came over about two. That means we'll be trapped up here for hours!"

Ben sat still. He thought of something he had heard Dad say often.

Stop panicking and try thinking.

"We don't have to just sit here," he said. "Maybe we can call out to somebody through those cracks where the light's coming in. But I think we'd better crawl along the beams. I don't know what's under the insulation. It might not be safe."

Hana eyed the insulation and refused to move.

"We might crash right through the ceiling and be killed," she said.

Ben gave her a look of disgust. Then he went ahead on his hands and knees. The beam was wide and perfectly safe. He made it to one of the gaps.

But when he tried to see through it, all he glimpsed was another bit of roof. Some light shone through the narrow crack, but he couldn't get his hand through it or see anything clearly.

"Help!" he called through the crack. "Help!"

His voice screeched up high like a baby's. He felt really dumb. Hana giggled. Still, it sounded better than her bawling, he told himself. He kept his back to her.

They both hushed and sat still, listening. Far, far away, Ben thought he heard a car horn. That was all.

"Try again," Hana told him.

"You try," he growled and backed up to let her by. But nobody heard Hana, either.

They got to three of the small gaps. Their shouts soon grew weak. Finally they crawled back to the trap door and sat there, staring at each other in the dim light.

Ben looked at his watch with the flashlight. It was hard to see. It was only five minutes past three.

"I knew I never should have come up here," Hana sniffed, on the verge of tears again.

Ben didn't answer. He was looking at his flashlight. Now he knew why he had had trouble seeing the time. The light was much dimmer. He was wearing out the batteries. He clicked the light off. The darkness seemed to press in around them.

"Turn it on," Hana cried. "It's too spooky up here in the dark."

Ben switched it back on. What would he say when Hana noticed that the beam of light was much weaker? He had no idea.

CHAPTER FOURTEEN

A Call for Help

They were trapped in the attic and Aunt Rose would not be home for nearly an hour. Ben's heart sank. Any second now, dumb old Hana was going to start bawling again.

He wanted to shake her. Why couldn't she make the best of things? If she'd just try . . .

That was what Dad had asked him to do. Had Dad wanted to shake him? Probably. He remembered his father's face looking at him yesterday. Ben swallowed hard.

Then he had an idea.

"Knock, knock," he said.

"What?"

"I said 'Knock, knock,' dummy. You're supposed to say . . ."

"I *know* what to say. Dummy yourself," Hana snapped. Then she added grumpily, "Who's there?"

"Ben."

"That's not a Knock, knock joke," Hana objected.

"Who says it isn't?" Ben asked. "Go on. Say 'Ben who?'"

"Ben who?"

"Ben to any good shows lately?"

Hana laughed. "That's not bad."

Ben grinned. He didn't tell her that Jimmy had made it up.

"You do one," he said instead.

They went through all the jokes and riddles they knew. Halfway through, when Hana was sounding happier, Ben explained about the batteries and turned the light off. Hana didn't like it. Neither did Ben, but he pretended he didn't mind. When they ran out of jokes, he switched it back on long enough to check the time. It was only twenty-two minutes past three.

For once, Hana came up with an idea.

"We could sing," she said.

Ben was not great at singing. Jimmy said he was always flat. But it was better than just sitting in the dark, waiting.

"You start," he told her.

She sang on and on. She knew all the hit songs. It turned out that she wanted to be a famous singer, as well as an animal trainer. Ben got tired of listening to her, but it was a lot better than hearing her cry. At least, he thought it was. After the sixth song, he wasn't so sure. He had a feeling Hana sang flat, too.

Finally four o'clock came. They leaned over the trap door opening, straining their ears. There was no noise from the house except a sound of distant music. Did that mean Aunt Rose had come home? Then Hana remembered turning the radio on for Gully. That was all it was.

The minutes crawled by. Hana had no more heart for singing. Ben could not think of a single riddle or joke. He was sick and tired of being up in that attic. He was thirsty and he needed to go to the bathroom.

At last they both heard a car door slam. It was a small, faraway sound, but they heard it. Ben went along the beam as fast as he could, in the direction of the sound.

"Aunt Rose, help!" he yelled. "We're trapped in the attic."

There was no answer. Ben scurried back to the trap door. They both listened. The noise from the radio got a bit louder. Had Aunt Rose turned up the volume? Hadn't she even noticed they were missing?

"Let's scream 'Help!' together. I'll count to three," Ben said. "One, two, three. *HELLLP*!"

They waited, holding their breath. Then Ben gave a groan.

"She thinks I'm over at your house. She told me to go there when I'd finished eating. She gave me a note for your mother. I stayed home because I wanted to come up here."

His voice trailed away miserably. Even though Hana was only a shadow in the darkness, he couldn't look at her.

"You mean she won't even miss you?" Hana demanded, her voice shrill.

There was a long silence. Then Ben heard Hana's breath catch in a sob.

"We'll be up here forever!" she whimpered.

Suddenly Ben remembered the note Aunt Rose had written for him to take to Mrs. Uchida. Where was it? Maybe he had left it on the kitchen table. She'd be sure to find it and guess something was wrong.

He opened his mouth to tell Hana. Then he changed his mind. Before he got her hopes up, he'd better check. He slid his hand into his right pocket. It was empty. Nothing in the left one, either. He found the scrunched-up piece of paper in his hip pocket. He left it there. He was glad he hadn't said anything.

"If only we hadn't shut both doors. If only I hadn't turned on the radio! Oh, Ben, maybe she'll never find us. I want to go home!"

"Who doesn't?" Ben muttered.

But another idea was coming to him. Hadn't he heard that dogs could hear better than people? He was sure he had. Somebody on TV had said that a dog's ears were seven times as sensitive as a person's. Maybe . . .

He swung over so he was lying on his stomach. He stuck his head down through the hole in the closet ceiling as far as it would go.

"Gully, come!" he called. "Gully, *come*! Gulliver Gallivant, we need you! *Come*!"

Hana stared at him. Then she caught on and joined him. They kept shouting and shouting. Then Ben put his hand on her arm.

"Let's listen," he said.

They listened with all four ears. And then, at long last, they heard a door opening. Next, before they could scream again, they both heard paws leaping at the closed bedroom door below them. And they heard Aunt Rose say, "Gully, don't be silly. There's nothing in there."

Ben couldn't understand why Hana had to start crying again at that point. They were safe. They didn't even have to shout again. The moment Aunt Rose opened the door, she saw the ladder. The next minute she was gazing up at them.

"What on earth . . ." she began.

Then Ben understood Hana better. Tears stung his eyes, too, at the sight of his aunt. He cleared his throat.

"We came up here exploring," he told her in a husky voice, "and we can't get down."

Aunt Rose climbed up the ladder and held onto them as first Hana and then Ben lowered themselves through the opening. The ladder did wobble a bit, but Aunt Rose didn't seem worried. She felt so strong and steady that Ben flung his arms around her neck and gave her a great hug.

Aunt Rose hugged him back with her free arm.

"Goose!" she said. "I never expected to find you up there. Gully kept running to the stairs and whining. Then he led me straight to the door. I wonder how he knew."

Ben smiled down at the dog.

"I called, 'Gully, come,'" he said. "And he did what he was told."

CHAPTER FIFTEEN

A Different Dragon

Gully was waiting at the foot of the ladder. He wagged his tail like mad when he saw Hana. But when Ben reached the ground, the dog seemed to go crazy with joy. He leaped up and licked Ben's chin. Ben shrank back against Aunt Rose and watched in horrified fascination as Gully shot off around the room in dizzy circles. Ben was sure he would crash into the wall at any moment, but Gully went whizzing around, just missing everything.

"What's wrong with him?" Ben demanded shakily.

Aunt Rose laughed.

"He's so pleased with himself that he can't stay still," she said. "Gully, you idiot, calm down."

She moved toward the speeding dog. Ben sprang after her for protection. Gully, swerving around her, found Ben directly in his path. The dog tried to stop in time but couldn't. He whammed one shoulder into the boy. Then Ben was flat on the floor with Gully peering down at him.

For one paralyzed second, Ben stared up at the dog looming over him. Gully's wide open mouth seemed enormous and full of jagged fangs. His great ribbon of a tongue practically touched Ben's nose. He felt Gully's hot breath fanning his face. All his terror of the huge dog came flooding back. He shut his eyes and waited for the dog to pounce.

"Come here, Gully, you big goof," Ben heard Hana say.

"This is between Ben and Gully," Aunt Rose said quietly. "You come with me, Hana. Your mother must be wondering where you are."

Ben, afraid to move or even breathe, could not believe they were deserting him. But then he heard their footsteps leave the room, Aunt Rose's swift, Hana's dragging a little.

He couldn't keep holding his breath any longer or he'd burst. He let it out gradually and waited. Nothing happened. Ben opened his eyes a crack. He was peering straight up into Gully's face. And Gully didn't look dangerous. He looked worried. Ben blinked and opened his eyes all the way.

The dog pawed Ben's arm then. It didn't hurt. It was like a nudge, commanding him to sit up.

Ben lay still for one more long moment. Gully's paw poked at him again. Gully also blew on him, a long whistling breath through his nose. It reminded Ben of a horse. Moving very cautiously, he rolled over and propped himself up on one elbow. Now he and Gully were almost eye to eye.

Whack, whack!

That was Gully's tail hitting the door frame. Then the dog sat down and reached out his paw. He poked at Ben's arm. He wanted to shake hands. He wanted to say he was sorry. It had all been a big mistake. Was that really what he wanted? It looked like it. Gully gave him another, harder poke.

"Okay, boy," Ben said. Then he took the big paw and shook it solemnly.

At once Gully jumped up, tail waving happily, paws frisking.

Moving carefully, Ben got to his feet. As he started for the door, the dog romping around him, he knew he would never be so afraid of Gully again. He still wasn't sure about dogs in general, but this big, silly dog liked him too much ever to want to hurt him.

When they reached the kitchen, they found that Hana had not gone yet.

"I was so scared up in that attic," she was saying to Aunt Rose. "It sounds dumb, but I thought we might be stuck up there all night. Ben wasn't half as scared as I was."

Aunt Rose grinned at Ben.

"He's like me," she said. "I didn't tell you before, Ben, but your father and I went up there once. We did manage to get down by ourselves, but it was only thanks to me that we did. Your dad kept crying and saying we couldn't. I remember that I really was scared myself, but I never let him know. One person in a panic was enough."

Ben stared at her, wide-eyed. Dad in a panic! He could hardly believe it.

"Did you get in trouble?" Hana asked.

"We sure did, and that was John's fault, too. He knocked down some of Grandma's things. She came home and caught us trying to put them back. I still remember the look she gave us. It was a humdinger."

Ben knew that look. Was that where Dad had learned it, from his grandmother?

Hana went home then. Ben helped get supper. Aunt Rose handed him Gully's dish and told him how much dog food to measure into it. When Ben leaned down with the dish, the dog's big head plunged in before he could set it down. In two seconds every last morsel had vanished.

Even though the Lab had just finished his supper, he wanted some of theirs. He kept putting up his nose and sniffing hungrily at the stove, right next to Aunt Rose. She dodged him for a few minutes. Then she turned to Ben again.

"See if you can make him lie down over there in the corner. I'm afraid I'll step on him or spill something hot over him."

She said it so matter-of-factly that Ben did not protest. He had already moved this dog from one spot to another, after all. And he had watched Hana. He took Gully's collar in his hand and tugged gently.

"Come on over here, boy," he said.

Gully came as meekly as a lamb. And when Ben said, "Down, Gully!" he flopped to the floor with a grunt.

All evening Gully trailed Aunt Rose and Ben around. But it was Ben's chair he lay down beside at supper.

When the three of them went for a walk, Aunt Rose held the leash. When she told Gully to heel, he walked beside her more or less calmly. It looked so easy that Ben was about to ask if he could take the leash for the last half block. Then the dog, seeing home ahead, speeded up and tugged Aunt Rose along until she had to use both hands to slow him down. Ben was glad he hadn't spoken.

Once they went back inside, though, and Aunt Rose was reading out loud in the living room, it was Ben's foot that Gully used for a pillow. Ben didn't say anything but he couldn't help noticing. He was pretty sure Aunt Rose noticed, too.

That was why the boy was not surprised when Gully followed him to the foot of the stairs at bedtime. Ben paused. He waited to see if Aunt Rose was going to call Gully back to her.

"Good night, boys," Aunt Rose said.

When Ben got into bed, Gully settled down on the mat next to the bunk. Ben lay on his side so he could watch the dog. Gully slept curled up in a ball, nose to tail. Ben thought about his family coming the next day. Boy, were they in for a shock!

CHAPTER SIXTEEN

Ben Decides

When Ben came down to breakfast on Sunday, Aunt Rose didn't say good morning. She burst into song instead.

"Just a few more hours before your folks arrive,
A few more hours, as sure as you're alive!"

Ben grinned at her. She was pretty smart, reading his mind like that.

"Why don't we have pancakes to celebrate?" she said next.

Ben's grin got even wider. He loved pancakes next best to spaghetti.

"Hey, we never ate that cream I whipped to butter," he remembered.

"It will taste perfect on pancakes, don't you think," his aunt said, "with lots of syrup on top?"

It tasted fine.

After they had finished, Ben took Gully out in

the yard. He wanted to see if he could get the dog to fetch for him the way he had for Hana. But before they could begin, Hana herself came running over.

"Come back inside. I've got something to tell you and Miss Tucker."

"But I'm just going to play with Gully," Ben protested. He looked at her sideways hoping he had surprised her.

"You can play later," Hana said in her bossiest voice. "Come inside now. This is important."

She ran toward the house, taking it for granted that he would follow. He had an urge to stay right where he was, but he was too curious. He followed her in. Gully came, too.

"Miss Tucker, guess what!" Hana began.

"You tell me. It's too early in the morning for guesses," Ben's aunt said.

"I'm going to be able to have Gully for my dog," Hana announced.

Ben felt shock jolt through him. Aunt Rose looked startled.

"Are you sure, Hana?" she said finally. "I was talking to your mother last night and she didn't say a word about changing her mind."

Hana reddened a little.

"Well, they did say I can have a dog," she said. "They still think Gully's too big. They want to get me a toy poodle. My mother doesn't want a dog that will shed hair on the furniture and my father says big dogs need too much exercise. But I just know I can make them change their minds, now that they've given in about letting me have a dog. I'll promise to brush him every day and walk him for hours and hours. When they know he has no place else to go, I'm sure they'll say it's okay."

The words ended abruptly as Hana ran out of breath and had to gasp for air. Aunt Rose couldn't help laughing. Hana looked hurt. And Ben, for some unknown reason, felt his heart start to sing.

"Hana, my sweet, a Labrador retriever is a far cry from a toy poodle," Ben's aunt said. "I'm sorry, but I don't think even you can talk your parents around that much. Labs shed hair in great gobs, even if you do brush them. And they do need more exercise than one eleven-year-old can possibly manage on her own. Besides, I'm pretty sure your mother is nervous around large dogs."

"Ben was scared of Gully, but he's changed," Hana argued.

Ben opened his mouth to protest, but stopped himself.

"Ben is one thing, your mother quite another. You know, Hana, poodles make wonderful pets. I know one that is just as good at retrieving as Gully. This dog chases after little balls and squeaky toys and brings them back over and over. It is every bit as big a pest as Gully."

Ben, watching Hana's face, thought he saw it brighten for one moment. Then the brief flicker of excitement died. She looked at Gully and sighed.

"I still think . . ."

"Don't. Give it up. Start getting pleased about a little dog instead. Gully just isn't meant for your family," Aunt Rose said firmly.

Hana looked stubborn.

"I don't see why you think Ben should have him then," she blurted, sticking out her bottom lip and glowering at Ben. "He hates dogs even more than my parents do."

Aunt Rose began putting away the clean breakfast dishes. She did not look at Ben.

"I think you already know why, Hana," she said over her shoulder. "For one thing, I know Gully belonged to a boy about Ben's age when he was a little puppy. I think he remembers. He certainly was drawn to Ben from the first. You must have noticed. Also, Ben's parents like large dogs. And his brother Jimmy has wanted a dog for years. He'll be pretty busy now with high school, but I know he'd love having a dog around. And Gully needs a family like Ben's. Those are my reasons. Now get along out of here, all of you, or I won't be ready for church on time."

When the three of them were outside again, Ben didn't know what to say to Hana. She looked grumpy. It wasn't his fault her parents wouldn't let her have Gully. So why was she mad at him?

"I've got to go," she muttered and took off.

He thought she wasn't even going to look back. Then she paused halfway up the back steps of her house, whirled around and shouted at him, "Goodbye. If you don't take him, you are out of your mind, Benjamin Tucker."

The door slammed shut behind her.

Gully did not let Ben stand staring after her for long. He fetched a large stick and thrust the spiky tip of it against Ben's limp hand. Ben got the message. He reached for it but, just in time, remembered to make Gully drop it first. Then he sent it skimming through the air. Gully fetched the stick over and over.

Once he did jump at it while Ben still had it in his hand. One of his teeth grazed Ben's thumb. Ben yelped and sucked his hand. Then he examined it for blood. The skin wasn't broken. All the same, he glared at the dog. He wasn't scared. He was just mad. Gully knew it. He sat down before Ben had a chance to scold him and held out his paw. Ben tried to look stern.

"You watch it, Gulliver," he growled. He shook Gully's paw up and down but forced himself not to smile while he did it. The big dope had to learn.

When Aunt Rose called them to come in, Ben felt as though they'd only been playing a few minutes. He glanced at the kitchen clock. He had actually been playing with a *dog* for three-quarters of an hour! A big dog, too.

They had to leave Gully behind while they went to church. Usually Ben found it hard to sit still during the boring bits in the service. But this time he hardly noticed them. He was too busy thinking. He tried imagining his family with a dog.

When there are storms, he thought, I could comfort him.

Gully met them at the front door. He jumped and danced around Ben, his tail wagging so hard it was a blur.

"It's a good thing I don't get my feelings hurt easily," Ben's aunt said. "That dog doesn't know I'm alive."

Ben was trying to fend off the excited Gully.

"Sit!" he bellowed.

Gully promptly sat, but he looked as though *his* feelings were hurt. Ben had to laugh.

He and Aunt Rose had lunch. Then he went up and read some more of the old comic books. Gully, looking bored, kept him company. Every so often Ben looked at his watch. Two-thirty. Three-twenty.

At last it was getting near the close of the afternoon. He got up and went to the landing at the head of the stairs.

Plop!

Something dropped at his feet. The old tennis ball. He gazed down at the dog's brown eyes.

"All right, you pest," Ben said.

He tossed the ball to the foot of the stairs. Away flew Gully after it. The two of them were so busy playing that they didn't even hear the front door open.

"Well, Ben," said Dad's voice, "I see you've slain a dragon after all."

Ben looked down at them, his family. Mum was beaming up at him. She had missed him, too. Jimmy was staring, his face blank with shock. But his father's eyes, warm with approval, were on Gully. Playing it cool, Ben bent down, picked up the ball and threw it again.

"He's not a dragon. He's my birthday present," Ben Tucker said.

Lost and Found

Contents

CHAPTER ONE

No Friends

Lucy Bell felt lost. She stood at the window of the Bells' new house and looked up and down the street. She saw some little boys out playing, but they were not even old enough to go to school. She did not see one girl her size. She did not see any girls at all.

Lucy leaned her head against the glass. She blinked to keep the tears back. Then she took off her glasses and cleaned them on her T-shirt. She put them back on her nose and sighed.

"What's wrong, Lucy?" asked Mrs. Bell.

Lucy did not turn around. She did not want her mother to see how sad she was. But her voice shook.

"I wish we still lived in Guelph. I don't know anyone in this town. There's nothing to do here."

"There's a lot to do," her mother told her. "There are all these boxes to unpack. There are your books and toys to put away. I need someone to go to the store for me, too. I forgot to get ice cream."

Lucy made a face.

"I don't want work to do. And I don't like putting things away. I want someone to play with. At home I had lots of friends. But here I have none. I'll never make a friend here."

Her mother shook her head.

"Lucy Bell, that's just plain silly. We only got here yesterday. It takes time to make friends. Give the girls here a chance."

"I don't see any girls here," Lucy said.

Mrs. Bell was sitting on the floor sorting through a box of sheets and towels. She got up and went to stand beside Lucy. They looked out at the street.

"Maybe they're still on vacation," she said. "Don't forget that this is the last long weekend of the summer. But school will start bright and early on Tuesday morning. They'll all be back in time for that."

She smiled down at Lucy, but Lucy did not feel like smiling. Her mother gave her shoulder a gentle shake.

"Don't worry. You'll soon have a friend. Now, how about helping me put things away?"

"I hate unpacking," said Lucy. "I'd rather go and get the ice cream."

"Well, let me make a list," Mrs. Bell said. "We do need some other things. Who knows? Maybe you'll find a friend on your way to the store."

Lucy felt happier as soon as she stepped outside. It was a sunny September day. There were no clouds in the blue sky. A warm wind ruffled her short red curls.

As she walked along, she looked for children her age. She saw a man cutting grass. She saw a woman shaking a mop out her back door. She did not see any girls or boys. But, three houses away from her own, she spotted a big tree with a swing on it. It was not a baby swing with arms. It was an old car tire hanging from a rope.

Lucy stopped walking. She looked at the yellow house that went with the swing. Nobody was at any of the windows. Quickly and quietly Lucy went over to the tree. She slipped into the tire and tried it out. Her feet just reached the ground. The child who owned the swing must be close to her size.

Lucy slid out of the tire and ran back to the sidewalk. The boy or girl who lived in that house might be home later today.

I hope it's a girl, Lucy said to herself.

She went on down Maple Road toward the store. It was very quiet. The only sound she could hear was the noise made by her own feet. No radios played. No dogs barked. No babies cried. It was as though everyone were under a spell like the people in Sleeping Beauty.

If only Kathy were here, Lucy thought, we could play at Sleeping Beauty.

Lucy missed Kathy most of all. Kathy had lived next door to her in Guelph. The two of them had been friends since kindergarten. Lucy gulped. She did not want to think about Kathy right now. She hurried into the store.

The store inside was a lot like the corner store in Guelph. A lady carrying a baby and a big bag of groceries was on her way out. Lucy held the door open for her. The lady gave her a big smile.

"Thanks, honey," she said.

Lucy smiled back. Then she began to look for the things on her list. She had to ask for the milk. The man behind the counter did not seem to notice she was new here. A lot of kids must come to his store.

Lucy looked over the candy. Her mother had said she could spend a dime on herself. She chose some licorice. When she had paid for everything, she put the change into the pocket of her jeans. Then she took a big bite of the licorice.

It tasted every bit as good as the licorice in Guelph.

When she was about halfway home, Lucy saw a

little white dog. He was running down a side street toward her.

He was a very small dog. He had fluffy white hair. His tail curled up over his back like a feathery plume. His ears were soft and floppy. Lucy had a hard time seeing his eyes, because they were half hidden behind a fringe of silky hair.

He made her think of a mop.

Yet from the very first moment she saw him, Lucy loved him.

CHAPTER TWO

Are You Lost?

When she first saw the little dog, Lucy looked to see who was with him. The side street was empty. The dog was so small that she thought he must be only a pup. He looked far too little to be out alone.

Lucy stood still and watched him. He was going up the street ahead of her. Each time he came to a front walk, he turned in. He ran halfway up to each house. Then he stopped short. He gave a worried little bark. Then, each time, he turned back and ran on to the next walk.

He must be lost, Lucy said to herself.

She hurried to catch up with him. When she did, she put down her bag of groceries. She went down on her knees. She held out her hand to the dog.

"Poor boy, are you lost?" she called to him softly. "Can't you find your home?"

The little dog stood still. He cocked his head to one side. He peered out at her from behind his shaggy fringe.

Lucy did not move.

"Here, boy," she coaxed. "I won't hurt you, boy."

She kept her hand held out to him. She stayed very still. She waited.

Slowly, so slowly, the little dog came to her waiting hand. He sniffed at her fingers. Lucy had never had a dog, but she knew how to make friends with one. She let him get to know her smell. Then she reached up and scratched behind his soft ears.

"You're a good boy," she told him. "Don't you belong here, either?"

The little dog was listening hard. Lucy went on talking.

"If you were mine, then neither of us would feel lost. I'd be your friend and you'd be mine."

The dog began to wag his tail. Then he got up on his hind legs and licked her chin.

Lucy thought she would burst. She put her arms right around the dog and gave him a hug.

"I love you, too," she told him. "You don't have a collar on. Maybe you're a stray."

She sat back on her heels and looked at the dog. She wanted him to look thin and dirty, as though he needed a home. Instead he seemed well fed and clean. Still, he was very small. It would not be right to leave him here. She made up her mind.

"You'll have to come home with me. I can't

leave you with nobody to look after you. You might get hit by a car. If you don't have a home, they might let me keep you."

She stood up and got the bag of groceries. Then, walking backwards, she started for home. The dog watched her, his head tilted a little. Then he ran after her.

Lucy turned around and ran. When she looked back, the little dog was at her heels.

Lucy ran on. She did not take time to look for girls her age. Even when she passed the house with the swing, she did not slow down. She did not see that this time, sitting on that swing, was a girl about her size. The girl saw Lucy. She stopped swinging. But Lucy and the little white dog flew past without noticing her.

Then they were in the Bells' front yard. The little dog was still right behind her. They went up onto the porch together.

"You wait here, boy," Lucy told him.

He looked up at her. Then he sat down to wait.

"You're so smart," Lucy said. "You understand every word I say."

He did not try to come in with her. She ran out to the kitchen and put the ice cream away. Then she hurried back to the front hall. Her mother was coming down the stairs. Lucy crossed her fingers.

"Guess what, Mum," she began.

"I can't guess. You tell me," her mother said.

"I've made a friend," Lucy told her. "You said I might find one on the way to the store. You were nearly right. I met him on the way home. He's outside right now."

"How nice!" Mrs. Bell said. "What's his name? Why didn't you bring him in?"

"He didn't tell me his name," Lucy laughed. "Come and meet him."

She opened the front door. Mrs. Bell looked out. There on the porch, right where Lucy had left him, sat the little white dog.

CHAPTER THREE

Trouble

The small dog on the Bells' front porch looked up at Lucy's mother. He tipped his head a little to one side. His tail quivered for a moment and then wagged hard. Mrs. Bell smiled.

"Oh, Lucy, what a dear little dog! Whose dog is he?"

"He's a stray," Lucy said firmly. "He doesn't belong to anybody. Please, Mum, may I keep him?"

Lucy's mother stopped smiling at the dog. She looked at Lucy instead.

"Lucy, you know better than that. You don't just bring somebody else's dog home and keep him."

"But he was lost!" Lucy stood very straight. "I couldn't just leave him."

"If he really was lost, his people must be looking for him this minute." Mrs. Bell's eyes were kind but her voice was firm. "You must take him right back where you found him."

Lucy took a deep breath.

"Mum, I didn't find him standing in one place. He was lost, honest. He was running along the street and he was scared. I'm sure he doesn't have a home. Nobody wants him but me!"

Lucy felt like yelling all this at her mother. She tried not to but her voice did grow loud. It began to shake, too. The little dog looked from her face to her mother's. He gave a small whimper.

"Poor boy," Mrs. Bell said.

She leaned down to pat him. At once he put his front paw up as if he wanted to shake hands. Mrs. Bell laughed. Lucy stopped wanting to yell.

"See, Mum, he likes you," she said. "He wants to stay with us. And he's just a baby. We have to take care of him."

Mrs. Bell put her arm around Lucy.

"Use your eyes, Lucy Bell. This is not a dog with no home," she said softly. "He's well fed. His coat is brushed. Someone has taken good care of him. I don't think he's just a puppy, either. He's a Maltese. They're toy dogs. They are very small even when they are fully grown. He's too well behaved to be only a baby." She frowned. "The one thing I can't understand is why he has no collar. A dog tag would help us to find his owner."

"Maybe his owner moved away and left him behind. Or maybe she's got another dog she loves better than him. She can't really love him. If she did, she wouldn't let him get lost."

Lucy's mother sighed. She stood back to let the little dog come into the house. Lucy's face grew bright with hope. Had her mum given in already?

Mrs. Bell had not.

"If nobody loved him, Lucy," she said, "he wouldn't be so friendly. Tell me the truth. Are you sure he was running loose? Did you coax him to follow you?"

Lucy looked down. She *had* called to him. But he *had* been running loose before she called. She was quite sure he did not belong where she had first seen him. She raised her chin. She faced her mother and told her the truth.

"He really was lost," she ended up.

"Well, he can stay until your father comes home, anyway. I have to get back to those boxes. Dad will be here soon. Then the three of us can talk it over. But don't get your hopes up, Lucy."

Mrs. Bell turned to go back up the stairs. Lucy did a little dance. The little dog wagged his tail. He jumped around her as if he were dancing, too.

"Can I give him something to eat?" she called to her mother.

"You can give him a drink of water. Put it in a bowl and leave it where he can help himself when he gets thirsty. But *do* try to remember that he has a good home and people who love him."

The little dog had a big drink of water. When he was done, Lucy ran up to her room. He followed her, just like the dogs on TV. She looked in her box of toys and found her bouncing ball. The two of them went back down to the living room. She could roll the ball for him there. He stood waiting to play, his eyes bright.

Lucy sat down on the floor and looked at him.

"I wish I knew your name. I wonder if I could guess it."

The little dog did not want her to guess his name. He wanted her to roll the ball. When she did, he tore after it. He ran back to her with the ball in his mouth. He put it into her hand.

"Oh, you're so smart," Lucy said. "I never saw such a smart dog."

He barked at her to roll the ball again. He fetched it ten times in a row. Then he sat down to rest.

Maybe now she could guess his name.

"Is your name Skipper?" she asked.

The little dog just sat there. She tried other names. Chum. Bingo. Snowy. Pal. Mopsy. Rumpelstiltskin. The dog lay down. He put his chin on his paws. None of those names was the right one. She would have to try again later.

A car door slammed. Her dad was home. Lucy

sat very still and wished. She had a feeling that if she wished very, very hard, her father might say she could keep the little dog. Then she would not mind having no friends here in Riverside. He would be her friend.

She heard her father's step outside the living-room door. She heard his voice.

"Lucy, your mother says you want to talk to me. What's the trouble?"

The little white dog jumped up. He raced to Lucy's father. He wagged his tail hard. He gave a quick high bark. Lucy stared at him. He couldn't know her dad already.

Mr. Bell squatted down and held out his hand.

"You're the trouble, are you?" he said, smiling at the excited dog.

The small white dog bounced up and down with joy. He looked from Mr. Bell to Lucy as if he wanted them to understand.

Then Lucy thought maybe she did understand.

"Trouble," she called. "Here, Trouble. Here, Trouble."

The small dog spun around. He raced over to her, ears flying. He jumped up at her. He licked her face. He knocked her glasses crooked. Lucy began to laugh.

"Dad," she said, "meet my new friend. I think his name is Trouble."

CHAPTER FOUR

Dad Makes a Call

Lucy's father liked Trouble. He sat and patted the dog while Lucy told him how she had found him. But when she said that Trouble was a stray with no home, her father shook his head just as her mother had done.

"Someone loves him," he said. "What if he were your dog? Think how you'd feel if he got lost. We must do our best to find his people."

Lucy did not want to listen.

"His people must be mean," she said. "If they loved him, why did they call him Trouble? He's no trouble."

Trouble looked pleased at the sound of his name. Lucy's dad laughed.

"A puppy is a lot of trouble," he said. "When Trouble was a pup, I'm sure he lived up to his name."

He gave Trouble one more pat. Then he stood up.

"I'll call the animal shelter. I'm sure someone must have phoned in to say he was lost."

Lucy knew that the animal shelter was a place where people looked after animals that were lost or hurt. She wished she knew of a way to keep her dad from making the call. But she did not.

Mr. Bell went to the phone. Lucy and Trouble stood beside him while he found the number. They watched him make the call. Lucy crossed her fingers. She held her breath while her father told about Trouble.

"Let us know if someone does call," he said into the telephone. "We'll keep him until somebody comes for him."

Lucy let out her breath in a sigh. Then her dad, turning from the phone, saw the smile on her face.

"Lucy, get used to the idea," he said. "Someone will miss Trouble and want him back. I have to go out again later. I'll get a newspaper. Maybe there will be something about him in the Lost and Found section."

But Lucy could not help hoping. Trouble loved her and she loved him. She was sure he wanted to stay.

"Why don't you take him out for a walk?" Mr. Bell said. "I have some rope you can use for a leash."

Soon Lucy and Trouble were going down the

front steps and along the sidewalk. This time, as she and Trouble came to the third house, Lucy looked over at the swing. Standing beside it was a girl, a girl only a little taller than Lucy.

CHAPTER FIVE

Nan

Lucy stopped walking and stared at the girl by the swing. She was eating a cookie. As she went on eating, she looked at Lucy. She looked at Trouble, too.

"Is that your dog?" she asked.

Lucy did not know what to say. She saw that the girl had long, straight, fair hair and bright blue eyes. She did not look very friendly.

"I said, is that your dog?" the girl repeated.

Lucy wished the girl had asked her something else. She looked down at Trouble.

"He's sort of mine," she said in a low voice. Then she talked on quickly. "We just moved here yesterday. I live in the house with the blue door. My name is Lucy Bell. What's yours?"

The girl finished her cookie. She stared hard at Lucy.

"What do you mean he's sort of your dog?" she said slowly.

Lucy put her shoulders back. She pushed her

glasses up on her nose. Her cheeks got red. So what if this girl was a bit taller than she was! Lucy had told what her name was. Now it was the other girl's turn.

"What's your name?" Lucy said again.

Suddenly the other girl smiled. Lucy liked her smile. Maybe she was nice after all.

"I'm Nan Greenwood," the girl said. "I saw you move in. You didn't have a dog yesterday."

Trouble pulled at the rope. He did not like to stand still. Lucy looked from him to Nan.

"I'm taking him for a walk," she said.

"I'll come, too," Nan said, as if Lucy had asked her. "Can I hold the rope?"

"No," Lucy said, her voice sharp. She thought fast. Then she added, "My dad says I have to hold it myself."

Nan looked surprised. Lucy was afraid she was going to ask why. But Nan had something else on her mind.

"Where did he come from?"

As they walked around the block, Lucy told her the whole story. Nan got excited right away.

"You mean he's a mystery? I love mysteries! I read mystery books all the time. I'm going to be a detective when I grow up. Maybe the dog belongs to some millionaire and he'll give you a big reward to get him back. I'll help you find out where he lives."

Nan's words came all in a rush. Lucy did not say anything. She did not want a big reward. She only wanted to keep Trouble.

Nan did not seem to notice how quiet Lucy was. She talked on.

"First we have to go back to the place where you found him and look for clues. We could question people, too. Let's go right now."

"I can't," Lucy said. "My mum said I could only go around the block. She needs me to help unpack. I'm supposed to go straight home."

Nan looked disappointed. Then she had another idea.

"I know something else we can do. We have yesterday's paper at home. Maybe somebody put something in the Lost and Found. It'll only take a second to look. Come *on*!"

Lucy ran in spite of herself. So did Trouble. Already Lucy could see that when Nan got an idea, it was hard to stop her. Lucy decided not to try. She might as well get it over with. If there was nothing in the paper about Trouble, she could tell Mum and Dad when she got home. Then they might give in and let her keep him.

"I'll bring the paper out here," Nan said when they reached the yellow house. "My mum's afraid of dogs."

She ran into the house. When she came back,

the two girls spread the paper out on the grass. The Lost and Found ads were at the back. When they found them, Nan gave Lucy a little push to one side.

"I'll read them out," she said.

Lucy stiffened.

"It's my paper," Nan said.

Lucy was angry. Who made Nan the boss? She could go home and read her own paper. She started to get up. Nan caught hold of her arm.

"We'll take turns reading," she said quickly. "You can go first if you want to."

Lucy sat back down. She looked at Nan's face. Nan did seem sorry.

"No, you go first," Lucy told her. "You're the one who wants to be a detective."

Nan bent over the paper.

"LOST ONE TABBY CAT NAMED COCO," she read out.

Then she got excited.

"Hey, listen to this one," she cried, forgetting to give Lucy her turn. "LOST," she read out, "ONE SMALL WHITE PUPPY"

Lucy sat bolt upright and stared at Nan. Nan rushed on.

". . . WEST HIGHLAND WHITE TERRIER BREED, MAY ANSWER TO SKIPPY."

Lucy sighed with relief. Nan paid no attention to this. She turned to where Trouble lay, his head on his paws. "Skippy," she called to him. "Skippy."

Trouble looked up at her from under his fringe without lifting his head.

"His name is Trouble," Lucy told her, "and he's a Maltese, not a West Highland White. My friend Kathy in Guelph has a Westie. They're a lot bigger than Trouble."

"It says that they'll give a reward," Nan said sadly. "Are you sure?"

Lucy nodded.

"It's my turn to read one," she said.

Nan looked from the paper to Lucy. Then she said in a very small voice, "That's all there are. The others are all found, not lost."

Lucy was so pleased, she did not care about missing her turn. She jumped to her feet.

"I have to go," she said. "Come on, Trouble. Mum needs us."

Trouble and Lucy ran across the grass.

"See you later, Nan," Lucy called back over her shoulder.

Nan dropped the paper. She jumped up, too, and began to run after them.

"Tell me where you found him," she shouted. "I can go and look for clues there by myself."

Lucy heard her but she did not turn her head. She and Trouble ran faster. Why did Nan want to be a detective, anyway? Well, she would have to think of some way to keep Nan from asking people about a lost Maltese named Trouble.

Because Trouble wanted to belong to her, Lucy Bell. She was absolutely sure about that.

CHAPTER SIX

Trouble's New Home

Lucy and Trouble ran all the way home from Nan's. When they got to the Bells' house, Lucy leaned against the front door. She was out of breath. Trouble's tongue hung out like a red ribbon. He looked as if he were laughing.

"We'd better go in and help Mum," Lucy said. "I told Nan we had to. If we do it, it will be almost true."

Trouble wagged his tail. They went in together.

Lucy and Trouble found Mrs. Bell in Lucy's room putting away her things.

"We came home to help," Lucy said.

"Good. I need all the help I can get," Mrs. Bell said. Then she looked at Lucy. "I saw you go by the house a few minutes ago with a girl your age. Have you found a friend after all?"

Lucy put her red knee socks in the top dresser

drawer. Was Nan going to be her friend? She was not sure.

"Her name is Nan Greenwood," she said at last. "She lives in that yellow house three doors up the street. She wants to be a detective when she grows up."

"A detective!" Lucy's mother sounded surprised.

Mrs. Bell left Lucy and Trouble to finish unpacking. When the things were in their right places, Lucy went downstairs and began to make a bed for Trouble. She got a heavy cardboard carton with no top. Mrs. Bell helped Lucy cut the side out with the butcher knife.

"Can I have something to put in the bottom to make it soft?" Lucy asked.

Her mother thought for a moment. Then she got some old towels she had used in packing. Lucy folded them so they just fit inside the bottom of the box. Then she took it up to her room and put it next to her own bed. The minute the box was in place, Trouble climbed into it. He turned around in a circle a couple of times. Then he lay down, all curled up in a ball. He looked up at Lucy.

"Mum," Lucy called, "come up and see something."

Her mother and father both came. When Mr. Bell saw Trouble lying there, he smiled. Then he looked at Lucy's happy face. He stopped smiling.

He spoke to her firmly.

"Lucy, don't get your heart set on keeping Trouble. I'm sure that dog has a good home. Remember, Lucy, Trouble is not yours."

Lucy did not know what to say. Why did they all want to take Trouble away from her? If he had such a good home, how had he got lost?

The phone rang. Lucy remembered the animal shelter. She bent down and put one hand on Trouble's head. She listened.

It was only Grandma. Lucy let out the breath she had been holding. She did not think any more about what Dad had said about not counting on keeping Trouble.

When she heard her mother hang up, she went down to ask if she could go and buy a can of dog food.

"Please, Mum," she said. "Please."

"But, Lucy . . . oh, well, all right. Just one tin, though."

Lucy and Trouble went out the back door. Lucy did not want to go past Nan's house. She felt sure that Nan would jump out at her and shout that she had found Trouble's real home.

Lucy looked over all the cans of dog food. She wished she knew which one the little dog liked best. At last she picked beef stew. She wanted to buy dog biscuits, too, but her mother had said she could just buy one tin of dog food. Then Lucy had an idea. She put back the small tin of beef stew and took down the large economy size instead. That would be enough to feed a little dog like Trouble for days and days.

"I'll get you the biscuits next time," she promised him.

When Lucy and Trouble got home, they met Mr. Bell in the hall.

"I want you to come with me, Lucy, to show me where you first saw Trouble. We can try asking people who live around there if they know him."

Lucy's heart sank. What if she said she could not remember? She took a quick look at her father's face. It would be no use. He would know it was not true.

Her mother came over and put her arm lightly around Lucy's shoulders.

"I need a rest from boxes," she said. "I'll come along for the ride."

Lucy could not say a word. She had too big a lump in her throat. Her feet dragged as she and the small white dog followed her father and mother out the door.

CHAPTER SEVEN

Nan Again

As the Bells and Trouble came out of the house, Lucy was so worried about losing the little dog that she did not notice the world around her. She jumped with surprise when a voice said loudly and clearly, "Hi, Lucy."

It was Nan. She was standing right next to Lucy's front walk. She was a little out of breath, as if she had come running the moment she had heard the Bells' door open.

"Hi," Lucy answered.

"Where are you going?" Nan asked.

Lucy wanted to tell her that was none of her business. It was bad enough that she had to go and ask people if they knew Trouble without having to tell Nan all about it first. Yet Nan's bright blue eyes were full of questions. And Nan was the only girl she had met here in Riverside. If Lucy had to give Trouble up, she was going to be more lost and lonely than before. She would need somebody. She took a deep breath.

"Mum, Dad," she said, "this is Nan Greenwood."

She watched her father and mother smile at Nan. They thought she and Nan were friends already. They were glad she knew someone her own age. Grown-ups often got things like this wrong.

"You must be the girl who wants to be a detective," Mr. Bell said.

Nan surprised Lucy by looking shy all at once. But she nodded.

"Then you should come along with us," Lucy's father said. "We could use a detective. We're going to try to find out who owns this little dog."

"Neat!" Nan said. "Can I really come? Will you wait while I ask my mum?"

Lucy did not say a word. Nan sped off to the yellow house. She was back in no time.

As Mr. Bell started the engine, Lucy sat very still with Trouble on her lap.

"Which way, Lucy?" her father asked.

Lucy cleared her throat. She told him. It was not far to where she had first seen Trouble. She pointed to the side street from which he had come. Her dad parked the car.

"We could have walked," he said. "Why didn't you tell us it was only three blocks?"

Lucy did not know what to say. She was glad when her father did not wait for an answer.

"Let's go," he said.

When they were all out on the sidewalk, he smiled at Nan.

"Keep your eyes open. You might spot a clue."

Lucy saw Nan grin back at him. She thought they both looked silly. Playing detective! How dumb. She wanted to kick them.

"Come on, Lucy, dear," her mother said softly. "Let's get it over with."

Lucy bent down and picked up Trouble. Her father was ringing the doorbell on the nearest house. Holding the little dog close, Lucy went to stand beside him.

"Would you like to ask the questions, Nan?" Mr. Bell said.

Lucy knew he was being nice because he thought Nan was her friend. Nan blushed a little. Her eyes sparkled with excitement.

"Sure," she said, "if you want me to."

Lucy said nothing. She did not feel friendly at all.

CHAPTER EIGHT

Is This Your Dog?

Mr. and Mrs. Bell, Nan and Lucy all stood looking at the house. It was a tall, thin house with long curtained windows. Trouble did not seem excited by it. Lucy's hopes rose.

An old man answered the door at last. He looked surprised when he saw four people and a dog on his doorstep.

"What can I do for you?" he asked.

"Go ahead," Mr. Bell said to Nan.

Nan pointed at Trouble.

"Is this your dog?" she said.

"That's no dog," the old man grinned. "That's a mop."

Nan blinked. Mr. and Mrs. Bell laughed. Lucy held Trouble tight. She knew that he did look like a mop. She had thought so herself. Still, it was mean of the old man to say Trouble was not a dog. He thought it was funny, Lucy knew. It did not seem very funny to her.

Nan was not laughing, either. Her face was red.

If she were a real grown-up detective, he would not make fun of her, Lucy thought. Over the top of Trouble's head, she glared at the man.

"I'm sorry," the man said. "No, that isn't my dog. I don't have a dog. I have three cats instead."

"Thank you," Nan said without smiling. She turned to go.

"Does anyone on this street have a dog like this, do you know?" Mr. Bell asked. "My daughter found him running loose near here and we want to find his home."

The man shook his head.

"Tina Marsh is the only one on this street with a dog. She lives in that red brick house at the corner. She has two dogs but they are big ones. Nobody's home over there right now, though. I saw their car drive off an hour ago. But I can tell you she has no little dogs."

"Thanks a lot," Mr. Bell said.

The old man stood inside his screen door and watched them turn to go. Lucy was the last to leave. She stayed behind for a minute putting Trouble down so that he could walk.

"You want to keep him, don't you?" the man asked her softly.

He did not sound mean at all now. The others were far enough ahead not to hear what he said.

Lucy nodded.

"Well, I hope you get your wish," said the old man. "He seems to be a nice little dog."

Lucy smiled.

"He is," she said. Then she and Trouble ran after the others.

They stood by the car. Mr. Bell looked at Nan.

"Now what shall we do?" he asked.

He spoke to her as if she were a grown-up. Lucy was glad. She liked the way her dad's words made Nan stand tall again.

"We should ask someone else," Nan said. "Maybe he doesn't know. Maybe he made a mistake."

"I don't think so," Mrs. Bell said. "I think he keeps an eye on his neighbours. He sounded very sure."

"It can't hurt to ask," Lucy's dad said.

They asked at two other houses. Nobody knew Trouble. Nobody had ever seen him before. When they came to the red brick house at the corner, Nan stopped.

"If this Tina likes dogs, she might know."

"The first man said there was nobody home there," Mrs. Bell reminded her.

"I can try anyway," Nan said.

She ran up the steps and rang the doorbell. They all heard dogs barking inside. They sounded like very large dogs. Trouble did not seem to like the sound of them. He did his best to pull Lucy back to the car. Nobody came to the door.

"We've done what we can here," Lucy's father said. "Let's go home."

Mr. Bell dropped Nan off at the yellow house.

"See you tomorrow, Lucy," Nan said.

Lucy waved her free hand. The other one was around Trouble. Nan looked at him through the open car window.

"Don't you worry, boy," she said. "I'll think of some way to find your home for you. So long."

She turned and ran inside. Lucy's father drove on.

"Nan seems like a nice girl," he said to Lucy over his shoulder.

Lucy looked down at the little white dog who was snuggled close beside her. She wanted to tell her father that right now Nan Greenwood was nothing but a pest. She wanted to say she would only like Nan if Nan would stop playing detective. She wanted to ask how she could get it into Nan's head that Trouble had a home with the Bells.

But she knew better.

"I guess Nan's all right," she said.

CHAPTER NINE

Trouble Settles In

"Lucy, would you please set the table?" Mrs. Bell said. "We're going to have an easy supper. I'm making waffles."

Lucy smiled. She liked waffles best of all. Even though she still was worried, Lucy cheered up. She sang as she got out the forks and plates.

"Oh, where, oh, where has my little dog gone?" she sang. "Oh, where, oh, where can he be?"

The song made her think of a boy or girl who might be looking for Trouble. She stopped singing. She looked for Trouble herself. He was not anywhere in the dining room or kitchen.

She found him in the hall. He was standing beside the front door. He looked at her as if he wanted her to open it for him.

"You're not lost now, Trouble," Lucy told him. "You're here with me. Remember the bed I made for you? You're going to sleep in my room."

Trouble did not wag his tail. He did not come to

her. He went on looking at the door. When she just stood there, he turned to her again. He gave one sharp bark.

"No, Trouble, no," Lucy whispered. "You're happy here. You want to stay."

She leaned over and picked him up. She carried him up the stairs to her room. She put him in his new bed.

"See, silly," she said. "That's where you're going to sleep."

The little dog stood there for a minute without moving. Then he sniffed all around inside the box. At last he lay down. But as soon as Lucy stepped back out of his way, Trouble jumped out of his nice bed and ran back down the stairs to stand by the front door.

Tears filled Lucy's eyes.

"Leave him be, Lucy," Mrs. Bell said. "He's not used to us yet. He'll be all right. Dad has checked the evening paper. There's nothing about a lost Maltese. So you can relax for a bit. Wash your hands for supper."

When the Bells sat down to eat, Trouble left the front door. He came straight to Lucy's chair. Then he sat up and begged. He liked waffles, too.

Lucy wanted to jump down and hug him. She broke off a bite of waffle for him instead.

"None of that, Lucy Bell," her father said. "He

must learn right from the start that he can't have food from the table."

Lucy felt mean.

"I'm sorry, boy," she said to the little dog.

"Trouble, get *down!*" Lucy's mother said in a sharp voice.

Trouble looked so sad that Lucy's heart ached. But he knew what Mrs. Bell's words meant. He stopped begging. He lay down and put his chin on his paws.

Lucy ate her waffles. As she ate, she thought about what her father had said. She could not remember his exact words. But he had said something like "he must learn right now that he will not be fed from the table." That sounded as if he thought Trouble might be going to stay.

If nobody calls tomorrow, she told herself, he'll be mine for sure.

When bedtime came, Lucy's mother read two chapters of *Ramona the Pest* out loud. Trouble lay in his bed next to Lucy's and seemed to listen. He looked as if he felt at home. But when Lucy's mother turned off the light and went downstairs, he got out of the box three times and went to the closed door. He scratched on it with his paw. Each time, Lucy hopped up and carried him back.

"This is your bed, Trouble," she told him. "Stay."

At last the little dog gave up. He curled himself into a ball and fell asleep with a tired sigh.

Lucy lay awake a little longer. Was it really only this afternoon that she had found Trouble? It seemed years and years since she had stood looking out the front window, feeling lost.

Lucy rolled over on her stomach. She reached out to touch the top of Trouble's silky head. It felt warm and alive under her hand.

CHAPTER TEN

Nan Finds a Clue

Trouble woke Lucy in the morning. He jumped up on her bed. He climbed on top of her. He licked the end of her nose.

"Oooof!" Lucy yelped. She pushed at him with both hands. "Get off me, you silly thing."

But she liked it, really. She sat up and hugged him. He wriggled free. He jumped down from the bed and ran to the door. He looked back at her and barked.

"I'm coming. Don't rush me," Lucy told him.

She reached for her glasses. Then she put on her clothes as fast as she could. Trouble barked again. She ran and got his rope. The two of them went for a run around the block.

As they passed the yellow house, Lucy looked for Nan. Was that her face at the upstairs window? Lucy waved and ran on.

"Your breakfast is ready and waiting," her father said as the two of them came in.

Lucy was eating her last bite of toast and honey when she heard a bang on the front door. Trouble barked and barked. He raced around in circles.

"Well, he's a good watchdog," Mr. Bell shouted over the noise. He went to the door. He was back in no time. Nan was right behind him.

"Look who I found on the doorstep," Mr. Bell said to Lucy with a smile.

Lucy had thought she did not want to see Nan this morning. But now she was glad after all. It was nice to know someone in Riverside. Maybe Nan would forget about looking for Trouble's home today. Maybe today Nan planned to be a doctor or a ballet dancer instead of a detective. Maybe they could play with their dolls.

But Nan had not changed. She had a piece of paper in her hand. She waved it in front of Lucy. Her blue eyes shone.

"I've found out!" Nan's words came in an excited rush. "I heard it over the radio. I wrote down the numbers. Here they are. I thought of it in bed last night."

"Slow down, Nan," Mr. Bell told her. "You're going too fast for us. What did you think of in bed last night?"

Nan looked surprised. She went on more slowly.

"I remembered that they tell about lost pets on the radio. So this morning I listened. And I was right! This is the phone number they gave and this is the house number. His name is really Tippy."

Lucy stared at Nan's happy face. She did not understand what Nan was saying. Who was Tippy?

Mr. Bell looked at Lucy. Then he took Nan by the arm and turned her to face him.

"Are you saying you know the phone number of Trouble's owner?"

Nan nodded. She held out the paper for him to see. Mr. Bell took it from her. He glanced at Lucy again. Then he reached out and picked up the telephone. Lucy could hear him dial the number. The room was so quiet that she could hear the phone ringing far away. Then a voice spoke.

To Lucy's surprise, her dad did not say anything. He hung up instead.

"Nan, you must have got the number wrong," he said. "They say there's no such number."

He looked at the slip of paper.

"Maybe I ought to try one more time. I may have made a mistake."

He tried again. The recorded voice still said there was no such number.

"Let's turn on the radio," Mrs. Bell said quickly. "They may give the number again and we can check it."

"The part about lost pets is over," Nan said in a low voice.

She stood first on one foot, then on the other. She twisted her hands behind her back.

"I thought I got the number right but I couldn't find a pencil," she admitted. "It only took me a minute but that must be why I got it wrong. I know the house number is right, though. It was easy to remember. It was 555 Bellwood Road."

Her face grew bright again. She looked at Mr. Bell.

"You see, it's your name and my name put together, sort of. We could go there and see, couldn't we?"

Lucy sat very still. She could not speak. She wanted to pick Trouble up and run and hide.

She saw her mother smile at Nan. "I can never find a pencil, either. John, why don't you take the girls and drive over to Bellwood Road? Do you know where it is, Nan?"

Nan looked proud of herself. "Yes. I can show you the way."

Lucy could not think why she had been glad to see Nan even for one moment.

Mr. Bell got Trouble's rope. The little dog jumped and danced around when he saw it. He was happy to be going out. Slowly Lucy got up off her chair. She took the rope from her father. She did not look at Nan.

"Come on, boy," she said. "Let's go for a drive."

Her back was very straight as she went out to the car.

CHAPTER ELEVEN

Tippy

Nan did know the way. Number 555 Bellwood Road was a grey stone house. Nan ran up the walk ahead of Lucy. She rang the bell.

Mr. Bell put his hands on Lucy's shoulders. They felt strong and steady. She wanted to lean back against him. She went on standing up straight.

"Chin up, Lucy," he said softly. "It'll soon be over."

The door opened. A teenage boy looked out through the screen. His hair was redder than Lucy's. He had lots more freckles, too.

"We brought your dog back," Nan told him. "We found Tippy for you."

The boy looked at her. He seemed not to know what she meant. Then he laughed.

"That's not Tippy," he said, looking at Trouble. "We already found Tippy. She was right next door all the time."

He turned away and shouted back into the house.

"It's some people with a dog." Then he called, "Tip! Here, Tippy."

A dog came running. She was much bigger than Trouble. She was very fat. She had pointed ears and a long skinny tail. And she had black spots! The tip of her tail was black, too. She barked loudly at Trouble.

"The radio said she was white with black spots," the boy said to Nan. "What made you think that was her?"

Nan hung her head.

"I was getting a pencil," she said in a small voice. "I didn't hear the part about spots."

"Well, we're glad you found her," Mr. Bell said to the boy. His hand was on Nan's shoulder now.

Lucy led the way back to the car. She was so happy that she even forgave Nan. She felt sorry for her. She touched Nan's hand.

"Never mind," she said.

Nan raised her head. She began to smile again.

"From now on," she said, "I will keep a pencil with me at all times!"

CHAPTER TWELVE

Friends

"Trouble and I are going over to Nan's, okay?" Lucy said when the lunch dishes were done.

"I thought you said Mrs. Greenwood doesn't like dogs. Maybe you should leave Trouble at home," Mrs. Bell said.

"Don't worry," Lucy said. "We can play outside. I can tie him up to their picnic table."

The phone rang. Lucy's heart beat fast. But it was only Nan.

"Bring your dolls," she said.

The girls sat at the picnic table. They dressed the dolls in their best clothes. Then they had a tea party. They used water for tea. Mrs. Greenwood let Nan have some little cookies shaped like animals. Trouble loved them. He ate a lion, two elephants and a bear. When the food was gone, he lay down close to Lucy. It was warm and sunny. Soon he was asleep.

Suddenly Nan got tired of playing with dolls.

"Why don't we go and ask some more people if they know Trouble?" she said. That girl Tina might be home now."

Lucy did not move. She had to make Nan understand. She spoke in a loud, clear voice.

"I don't want to ask anyone about him anymore. I want him to be mine. If he has a home, it must be a bad home. Good people wouldn't have let him get lost."

Nan stared at her. She opened her mouth to argue. Lucy stood up. She gave Nan a hard, straight look. This time she was not going to go along while Nan played detective.

Nan sighed.

"All right," she said. "Never mind . . . let's play Fish."

Lucy sat down again. She felt like dancing. Nan was not going to pester her any longer about looking for clues. They were going to play Fish instead.

Lucy loved playing Fish.

Nan went into the house and came back with a deck of cards. Lucy hoped the other girl would not ask her to shuffle. Shuffling was the one thing Lucy did not like about playing Fish. She was no good at it. Would Nan laugh at her if she dropped the cards?

For the first time, Lucy was glad that Nan was the kind of girl who did not like taking turns.

She watched Nan start to shuffle. Nan was not so good at it, either. She dropped some cards. She picked them up without a word. She tried to go faster. Then she dropped almost all of them.

"I can't shuffle very well," she said, her cheeks pink.

"Me, neither," Lucy told her. "Sometimes I drop every single one."

Nan looked much happier. She started to give the cards out. Then she stopped and looked across at Lucy.

"What if Trouble's people do come for him?" she asked. "Will your mother and father let you get another dog?"

"I don't want any other dog." Lucy's voice was sharp. She bent her head over the cards in her hands. "Have you any kings?"

Nan looked at the red curls on the top of Lucy's head.

"Fish!" she said.

They played for a long time. After three games of Fish, they played Snap and Concentration. Nan was faster so she won the game of Snap. But Lucy had a better memory. She beat Nan easily at Concentration.

"Barbara Christie is coming back from their cottage tomorrow," Nan said at last, putting the cards down.

"Who's Barbara Christie?"

"I thought I told you already. She's my best friend," Nan explained. "Her birthday is the day after Christmas. She lives next door to you in that double house. The Christies live in the ground floor apartment on the left side."

Lucy gathered up her cards and put them into a neat little pile. She did not look at Nan. She had hoped she was going to be Nan's best friend. Maybe this Barbara would be nice, though. Maybe the three of them could be friends.

Anyway, if Barbara doesn't like me, she told herself, I'll still have Trouble.

She stood up.

"Let's take Trouble for a walk," she said. "I'm sick of playing cards."

The three of them raced until they were out of breath. Nan told Lucy more about Barbara Christie then. She had a white mouse called Nosey. She and Nan were going into Mr. Good's class.

Lucy gave a little skip.

"I'm going to be in his class, too," she told Nan. "My mother got a letter."

She looked to see how Nan would feel about that.

"Neat," Nan said. "Barbara thinks we should start a club. Did I tell you that she wears glasses just like you?"

Lucy wanted to twirl around and around until she was dizzy. Instead she began to run again. The three of them raced back to Nan's house. Trouble won.

"Nan, come in and get washed. It's almost suppertime," Mrs. Greenwood called.

Lucy was surprised. She had thought suppertime was a long way off. She skipped home. Trouble bounced along beside her. She would not mind starting school the day after tomorrow. Nan and Barbara would walk with her. And they would start a club.

She opened the front door and went in. The phone was ringing. Her father answered it.

"We'll be right over," he said.

He hung up slowly. He looked at Lucy.

"That was the animal shelter," he said. "Trouble's people are there. I'm sorry, Lucy," he said. "I really am."

CHAPTER THIRTEEN

Andy

Mr. and Mrs. Bell, Lucy and Trouble drove to the animal shelter. Lucy was glad her mum was there. Tears ran down her face.

Lucy's glasses got misty. Her mother took them off. She put them in her handbag. Lucy cried on.

She had been so sure that Trouble was hers now.

She held Trouble close. He did not like her to cry. He wriggled free. He put his front paws on her shoulders. He licked some of the tears off her face.

"Lucy, dear, stop," her mother said gently. "Look at poor Trouble. He doesn't understand. He's worried."

Lucy gulped back a sob. Mrs. Bell took a handkerchief from her pocket and handed it to Lucy.

Mr. Bell was driving slowly, looking for the animal shelter. They came to a long, low building.

"I think this must be the place," Lucy's father said.

Lucy's mother got out of the car. She reached to

take Trouble from Lucy. But Lucy would not let her have him. Somehow she got herself out with Trouble still clasped in her arms.

She started up the walk between her mother and father.

She had made up her mind. She was not going to give Trouble back to people who did not love him. She would not do it, no matter what anyone said.

I'll ask them how come they let him get lost, she thought. I'll ask them why they didn't call the animal shelter sooner. I'll ask them to sell him to us!

That would work! That was a great idea! If only she had thought of it sooner. Now it was too late to tell her father and mother. Her dad was already opening the glass door of the building. She followed her mother inside.

Lucy could not see clearly without her glasses. The front office of the animal shelter seemed to be full of people. Had they all come about Trouble?

Then she heard a boy's voice.

"It *is!* It's Trouble! Oh, Trouble, I'm back. It's all right. I've found you!"

Then Lucy could not hold onto Trouble. He struggled to get loose. His tail whacked against her. He gave little yips of joy.

Lucy had to let him go. She saw the boy now. He was down on his knees. The minute she put Trouble down, he flew into the boy's arms.

Lucy did not want to believe it. But she had to. The Bells were not going to be able to buy Trouble. It was no use even asking. These people would not sell him.

Even Lucy could see that this boy and this dog loved each other.

Trouble barked like mad. The boy did not tell him to be quiet. The boy was not saying anything now. Lucy felt something touch her hand. Her mother was giving her back her glasses. She put them on and looked at the boy, seeing him clearly for the first time. Then she understood why he was not saying a word. He was crying.

Lucy stood and watched him. He was big. Lucy thought he must be twelve or thirteen. Yet he was crying too hard to talk.

He doesn't even know we're here, she thought. The only one he sees is Trouble.

And Trouble only sees him, a voice inside her said.

CHAPTER FOURTEEN

Tina

"We only found out that Andy's dog was missing about an hour ago," the boy's father was saying to Mr. Bell. "We went to spend the weekend with my sister in Toronto. She has a cat with new kittens so we left Trouble behind. Andy didn't want to leave him in a kennel. He was sure the dog would be much happier with his friend Tina."

He stopped talking to look at a girl who was with them. Lucy looked at her, too. She remembered the old man telling them about a girl named Tina, Tina Marsh. That Tina had had two big dogs but no small one. Nan had rung her doorbell but only the dogs had been home.

The girl's eyes were red. But she was not crying now. She was looking at Andy and Trouble and she was smiling.

"I didn't mean to lose him," Tina said. She talked fast. Her voice was unsteady, as though any minute she might begin to cry again.

"My dogs, Nip and Tuck, needed a bath. I thought I would give Trouble a bath, too. It would be a surprise for Andy. I took off their collars. I thought I'd do the big dogs first."

Tina stopped to take a breath. She was looking straight at Lucy.

"It was a nice day so I left Tuck and Trouble out in the yard," she hurried on. "I didn't know there was a hole in the fence. It was such a little hole I didn't notice it. But when I went to get Tuck, Trouble was gone. I called and called him. I couldn't believe he was really lost. I looked everywhere in the house and yard first. I told myself he wouldn't run away, not from me. He likes me."

Lucy saw that all the grown-ups were feeling sorry for Tina. But Lucy was not sorry. She spoke up in a voice so loud it surprised even her.

"You didn't call the animal shelter. I found him yesterday afternoon. That's a long time ago. He could have been run over."

Her voice began to shake. Tina hung her head.

"I kept hoping I could find him somehow." Tina spoke in such a low voice that they had trouble hearing it. "I thought he would go home. Dogs in books always do. I really wanted to find him before Andy came back."

Andy's father patted her on the back.

"It's all right, Tina. He's found now. That's what counts."

Nan said we should talk to Tina, Lucy thought. She was right all along.

Then Andy's father looked at Mr. and Mrs. Bell.

"I'd like to give your daughter something for finding him and taking such good care of him," he said. "Andy thinks a lot of Trouble. You can see that. It was good of you to look after the dog till we showed up."

"Well, Lucy, what do you say to that?" her father asked.

Lucy looked at Trouble. He was so happy to see Andy that he had not once looked back at her.

"I don't want anything," she said. "It was . . . it . . ."

She was going to say that it had been fun looking after him, but she could not get the words out. She held her head up.

"Good-bye, Trouble," she whispered.

Then she had to get away. The front was crowded with the Bells, Andy's parents, Tina, the man from the animal shelter. She looked around for a way out. Nearby was a door that stood open a little. Lucy ran through it. She found herself in a narrow, empty hallway. There were a couple of other doors, but they were shut. Lucy stood still and waited. Nobody followed her. She heard them beginning to talk again. She was safe.

Then Lucy leaned against the door, snatched off her glasses and let the tears come.

CHAPTER FIFTEEN

The Sad Dog

Lucy felt as though she were going to cry for a long time. She did not think she would be able to stop until she was at home. She did not want any supper. She just wanted to get into her own bed and cry herself to sleep.

As she thought of her room, she remembered Trouble's box. Sobs choked her.

Suddenly, from the other side of the door, she heard something go "Woof!"

Lucy gasped. That one bark was just the beginning. In two seconds it sounded as though every dog in Riverside was barking at her through the closed door.

Using both hands, Lucy rubbed away her tears. She jammed her glasses back on. She eased the door open. Inside was a dimly lit room lined with cages. Most of them had animals in them.

They must be the lost or hurt ones that found shelter here.

Lucy leaned down and looked through the wire net on the front of the cage nearest to her. There were three small black puppies inside. They were all barking at her!

"Hush," Lucy said.

As if they understood her, they stopped barking and began to play. They chased each other around the box. They fell over their own feet. Two of them tried to box. The third one knocked the first two down and sat on their heads.

Lucy laughed. The tears dried on her cheeks.

She moved on to the next cage. She saw a mother cat with two tiny kittens. They were so small that their eyes were not open yet. Lucy watched the mother cat feed them.

She went on down the row. A few cages were empty. There were lots more kittens. She saw more pups, too. One white puppy made her think of Trouble.

She looked at the door leading to the front office. Had Andy gone? She heard an outside door shut.

Lucy went back to watching the white puppy. He sat down suddenly. He yawned. He bit his tail. Then he went to sleep.

He would not know tricks the way Trouble did. Lucy thought of Trouble putting out his paw to shake hands, running and fetching her bouncing ball, sitting up and begging for a bite of waffle. Andy had taught Trouble so much.

Lucy swallowed and blinked away new tears.

"You're a nice pup," she said, putting her fingertips through the holes in the wire net. The puppy did not wake up.

Then she saw another dog.

It was a tiny dog, smaller than Trouble even. It looked like a fox cub. Its coat was a golden brown, like a fall leaf. It did not peer out from behind a fringe of hair like Trouble. It had a neat little head with perky ears. Lucy could see that the fur of its chest was soft and creamy white.

Yet none of this was what made it so different.

It lay very still. It would not look at her. It was staring at the wall of its cage. It had big, sad-looking eyes. Even though it was so small, Lucy was sure this dog was not a puppy. Puppies were playful. Puppies did not look so lonely.

Lucy tapped the door of the cage softly. She tried to whistle. The puppies in the nearby cages yipped fiercely at her. The sad dog did not turn its head.

It made her think of Trouble waiting by the door, waiting to go home.

"Hello," she said in a soft voice. "Hello, little dog."

It looked at her then. For one moment it came

alive with hope. Then it saw she was a stranger. It turned away. It grew limp again. It went back to staring at nothing.

"Well, Lucy, that's over," her father said behind her. "I was proud of you for not taking a reward. Your mother and I have been talking. We'll get you a new puppy tomorrow. You'll soon love it even more than Trouble. Now let's go home."

Lucy stayed where she was. She looked back down the row of cages. She saw all the puppies, big and little. They were cute. They were covered with baby fluff. Any one of them would be fun to have, fun to teach, fun to cuddle. The white one still made her think of Trouble.

Then she looked back at the small sad dog.

"Is this a lost dog?" she asked the animal shelter man. 'Will someone be coming to take this little dog home?"

CHAPTER SIXTEEN

Missy

The three Bells were all looking at the sad dog now. The man from the animal shelter moved to stand next to Lucy.

"She's not lost," he said, "but she has no home. She's a toy Pomeranian. Poms they call them."

Mrs. Bell looked at the still little dog.

"Where did she come from?" she asked quietly.

"It's a sad story." The man was watching Lucy as he spoke. "She belonged to a little girl about the size of your daughter. The child loved the dog very much. Then her little brother grew to be allergic to dog hair. The doctor said they had to get rid of the dog. It was hard for the little girl. But she understood why. The dog doesn't."

He undid the latch on the front of the cage. He reached in and picked up the tiny dog. He held her against his big chest. He patted her. The dog lay very still in his arms. She did not look at anyone.

"She's five years old," the man told them. "She

has lived in that home all her life. They couldn't find anyone to take her. I said that she wasn't lost. I was wrong. She's more lost than that boy's dog. They left her here a week ago and she's been like this ever since. I think she knows they aren't coming back."

"If she were happy, she'd be beautiful," Lucy's mother said. "She's so delicate."

"I think you're waiting for us to go so you can close this place up for the night," Mr. Bell said to the man.

The man did not answer. He was watching Lucy. Mr. Bell looked at her, too. Lucy looked only at the sad little dog.

"What will happen to her?" she asked.

"We'll try to find a home for her. Most people want puppies. But I'm sure someone will take her because she's an expensive dog. Whoever takes her will have to be kind and patient to win her heart."

Lucy stretched out her hands. She took the dog into them.

"I would be kind to her," she half whispered.

She cuddled the Pom close. She looked into the lonesome dark eyes. Very gently she stroked the red-gold fur.

"Why, Lucy, her hair is almost the same colour as yours," her mother said.

Lucy looked up at the man. He was smiling at her.

"Do you know her name?" she asked him.

"Missy, I think. He looked at a tag on the front of the cage. Lucy had not noticed it before.

"That's right. Missy," he told her.

"Lucy, that dog would never be all yours," said her father, breaking in. 'We'll get you a Maltese puppy like Trouble. I'll get him first thing tomorrow. You don't want a dog with a broken heart."

Lucy stood looking at him. Was he right? Wouldn't a Maltese puppy be better?

Then Missy made up Lucy's mind. She did not lift her head to lick Lucy's cheek. She did not look happy. She just moved a tiny bit. She moved closer to Lucy. She pushed her head up under Lucy's chin. She rested it against Lucy's neck. She gave a small sigh.

Lucy ducked her head down so that she could speak into the dog's ear.

"Missy," she murmured, "oh, Missy."

Then she looked up at her mother and father. She saw her mother smile. She saw her father looking worried.

"Can Missy and I wait out in the car?" she asked them.

Neither Mr. nor Mrs. Bell said a word. They just nodded.

"Good girl," the man from the animal shelter said softly.

Lucy was not sure whether he meant Missy or herself. She did not stay to ask.

When she and Missy were by themselves in the car, she put her cheek down on the top of the dog's head.

"I'm lonely, too, Missy," she said almost in a whisper. "Trouble is gone. And I don't know if Nan and Barbara will be my friends. So I know how you feel. But it'll be all right. You and I will be friends with each other. After awhile, you won't be sad any more. Because you know what? I love you already, Missy."

At that, Missy's tail, which had hung so limply, curled up. And Lucy felt the tip of it wag ever so slightly against her bare arm.

CHAPTER SEVENTEEN

The Right Question

It was Monday afternoon. Nan and Lucy were out on the Bells' front porch. They were playing Fish again. Nan kept stopping to look at Missy.

"She's not much like Trouble," she said. "He was so friendly."

"I know," Lucy said.

She did not tell Nan that when she had wakened that morning, she had found Missy curled up beside her. She had not felt the dog jump up onto the bed. Trouble had never cuddled up close to her like that. She was tired of hearing that Missy was not like Trouble. Nan had said it three times so far.

"I want all your threes," Lucy said.

Nan gave her two cards.

"I wish Barbara would come home," Nan said then. "I thought they would be here by now."

Nan kept saying that over and over, too. Lucy sighed. It was hard to play Fish with Nan today. She kept talking about other things.

"Do you have any nines?" Lucy asked.

Nan did not answer.

"Nines," Lucy said again. "I want your nines."

Nan still did not answer. Lucy looked up. She saw Nan scramble to her feet. Her cards fell to the porch floor.

"Look! There's Barbara!" she shouted. "She's back!"

She dashed down the steps. She ran across the grass. Her long hair flew out behind her. She stopped beside a car full of people. A girl got out.

Missy had been lying near Lucy. Now she raced back and forth on the porch. She made little sounds deep in her throat. Lucy watched her. Missy had not barked once since they had brought her home. She had been too good. Too quiet. She had acted like company. Was she going to bark now?

"Hey, Barbara, I thought you'd never get here," Nan said in an excited voice.

And Missy began to bark. She yipped and yapped. She ran over and jumped up against Lucy who was still sitting cross-legged on the porch floor. She ran back to the top of the steps. She was watching Nan.

Lucy laughed. She got to her feet, too. She stooped and put a hand on Missy's back.

"Be quiet," she said. "Missy, quietl"

Missy gave one more bark. Then she stood, ears

forward, eyes bright, staring down at Nan and the new girl.

Lucy looked, too. Barbara was not as tall as Nan. She had short brown hair. Lucy could see her glasses.

Nan was bringing her over.

"This is Lucy, Lucy Bell," Nan said. "She's going to be in our class. I told her all about you."

The two girls were at the bottom of the porch steps. Lucy stood and looked down at them. Her face felt hot. She wished Nan had waited a little before bringing Barbara over. What was she supposed to say? She did her best to smile.

"Hi," she said. "Nan told me you were coming."

The words sounded dumb. Lucy wanted to run and hide. At last Barbara spoke.

"What a cute little dog!" she said. "Is it yours?"

Lucy remembered when Nan had asked her the same question. She had asked it about Trouble. It had been the wrong question to ask then. But now everything was different. Barbara's question was exactly right. Lucy felt happy clear down to her toes.

She leaned down. Gently she lifted Missy up into her arms. She smiled at Barbara over the top of the little dog's head.

"Yes," said Lucy Bell proudly. "Missy is mine."

One to Grow On

Contents

CHAPTER ONE

One Sunday Morning

"I don't want to go," Janie said.

Mother picked up the plastic measuring spoons Tim had just flung out of his playpen and handed them back to him politely. Tim grinned up at her and stamped his feet like a pony.

"You're quite welcome, Timothy," she told him, "but don't do it again. You're much too old for that sort of thing."

"Moth-er!" Janie's voice rose angrily.

But Mary Chisholm had moved. She was at the foot of the back stairs calling instructions up to the two teen-agers who had not yet come down.

"Elaine! Rob! If you want anything to eat this morning, you have exactly three minutes to get down here."

Janie wanted to stamp *her* foot. It was always like this, trying to talk to Mother. She was harder to catch than a diesel locomotive. Now she was plugging in the coffeepot, turning on the tap and running the dishwater, getting out Dad's grapefruit, pouring juice for Rob and Elaine, getting Tim a square of toast . . .

"Stephanie Jane Chisholm," her mother said, rounding on her suddenly and speaking in a voice edged with irritation to match Janie's own, "why must you stand right in the middle of the floor? You couldn't be more in my way if you tried."

"If you ever listened to me, you'd know!" Janie exploded. "I've been trying to tell you something for *hours*. I've tried at least *five* times—but you never hear one word."

"You've tried once. Maybe twice, Janie. And it hasn't been 'hours.' You've been out here for only about ten minutes all told."

"It's been longer than that," Janie said weakly.

Mother shook her head. Then she began, once again, to say the words Janie had heard so often.

"Janie, when will you learn to stop exaggerating everything so. It's time you grew up and started sticking to the truth."

"But you *don't* listen . . ." Janie interrupted.

"I do," Mary Chisholm answered crisply. She was stacking her own and Janie's breakfast dishes as she spoke. Suddenly, she looked up, hearing her husband coming down the front stairs. Janie, catching the sound of his step an instant later, regarded her mother with admiration. Always, Mother heard him first.

"I am listening right now," Mother went on, picking up the grapefruit and starting in to the dining room. "I even know what it is you've been trying to tell me for 'hours' . . ."

"You don't want to go to Sunday School," she finished triumphantly, setting the half grapefruit down at her husband's place.

Dad, pulling his chair in to the table, gave her a startled glance.

"Sunday School," he echoed blankly. "Why would I want . . ."

"Don't be silly, Jim. I'm talking to Janie. She's the one who doesn't want to go to Sunday School."

"Why?" Dad asked.

Janie opened her mouth to explain but Mother beat her to it.

"Because she's the one and only person in this house who has to go—at least until Tim's a couple of years older."

Janie felt a little like a pricked balloon but she was not ready to retreat yet.

"Well, it's true," she asserted.

"Hmph," her father said and disappeared into the weekend paper.

Janie thought of telling him that he never

listened either. Then she had to smile. He would not even hear her say that much. Yet, somehow, that was all right. That was just the way Dad was. She would not want him changed. Mother was different. If Mother, just once, would pay attention . . .

Mother brought the coffeepot in and put it where her husband could reach it. Then she returned to the kitchen. Janie followed her, as determined as a bloodhound.

"There are seven people in this family," she told her mother. She spoke each word slowly, so that her mother would feel the full weight of this argument. "There's Dad and you and David and Elaine and Rob and Tim and me . . ."

"And five of us are too old for Sunday School and one is too young—and that leaves one—you!" Mother countered neatly. "Call Elaine and Rob again, will you please, dear? Tim, stop being a fire engine for a moment. I can't hear myself think. Ask Elaine if she's made her bed. No, never mind. I'll do my own asking. . . . But, speaking of beds, is yours made?"

"Yes, it is," Janie said proudly, her voice sure, her chin high.

It was so nearly true that, for an instant, she believed it herself. She *had* started to make it, after all. She had pulled the covers up and was beginning to straighten them when she had remembered it was Sunday and she had gone to find her lesson book and then, she had stopped for breakfast, and then . . .

"Good for you, Janie," Mother said warmly, giving her a real smile.

Janie squirmed. But it would be all right. She would just slip upstairs and do it before Mother learned the truth. She . . .

"Janie, I told you to call Rob and Elaine," Mother reminded her.

Elaine came clattering down.

"I'm here," she told Janie. "And my bed's made," she added to her mother. "Rob's still sleeping."

"Rob!" Janie bellowed up the back stairs.

"Okay, okay," Rob returned in a foggy voice. His feet thudded on the fioor above her. "I'm coming. Tell Mom I want bacon."

Mother heard, shook her head over her son's manners, said "please" for him and opened the refrigerator door.

"Thank goodness David's not like that!" Janie exclaimed.

"Oh, David's not perfect. You've forgotten what he was like when he was Rob's age," Mother answered.

But she smiled again, just speaking David's name.

Janie understood the smile. David, at nineteen,

was the eldest. That made him special. He was special, too, because he had gone away from them into a world of his own. He had just finished his first year in college and now he was in Riverside working for Andrew Copeland, a friend of Dad's, for the summer. Janie knew that her parents were proud of him. She, Janie, did not care about his good grades or the "fine experience" he was having in Riverside. She simply wanted him home where she could get to him when she needed him. David did listen.

"Nobody else is like David," she said huskily to her mother.

"Why, Janie, you and David are as alike as two peas in a pod," Mother said.

Janie stared at her.

"Me . . . like David?"

Mary Chisholm laughed. She went on putting bacon strips into the frying pan.

"When David was your age, he used to argue, for no good reason, just the way you do. And for years he's been after me to 'stop and listen'. Then, he goes off into his own thoughts and forgets the rest of us are there. You do that too. You both swoop from happiness to misery and back again in no time flat. I don't know where you get it from. Your father and I—and Elaine and Rob, too, for that matter—are so much more of a piece. You and

David—I don't know what's going on inside you, half the time," Mother admitted.

Janie was fascinated.

"Did David . . ." she began eagerly.

"Did David what?" Mother probed when Janie halted in mid-sentence.

But Rob was there, all at once. And Elaine and Dad were placing their orders for bacon too.

"Nothing," Janie muttered.

She was sure, anyway, that David had not told lies when he was her age. Time was passing. Remembering her unmade bed, Janie tried to fade quietly out of sight.

"Janie, you still have twenty minutes. You could get started on those dishes," Mother said firmly.

Janie hurried but twenty minutes was not long enough.

"Heavens, Stephanie Jane, you're going to be late," Mother cried, catching sight of the clock.

She hustled Janie into hat and gloves, giving her no chance to talk. On her way to the front door, she did make one last half-hearted attempt to rebel.

"What if I just won't go?" she asked. "What if I go on strike and lie on the floor and refuse to move . . ."

"Jane Chisholm, stop talking nonsense and *hurry!*"

But before Mother had Janie safely through the

door, the phone rang. Mother reached for the receiver. Janie halted, not really meaning to listen, just dawdling for a moment to show she was free to do what she pleased.

"Tilly!" Mother said happily—and Janie changed her mind about listening.

After all, Matilda Barry was Janie's godmother as well as Mother's closest friend. Tilly probably wanted to speak to her, Janie.

"Yes, Janie's right here—but she's on her way out the door to Sunday School and she's going to be late," Mother said.

She eyed Janie sternly as she spoke and waved "Good-bye." Janie stood her ground.

"Hold the line, for a minute, Tilly . . . Janie, go *on!*"

"But maybe Tilly . . ."

"Never you mind about Tilly. If she has any messages for you, I'll tell you at lunch. Now, march."

Janie leaned forward swiftly and spoke directly into the receiver in her mother's hand.

"Hi, Tilly."

Tilly's deep chuckle reached her.

"Hello, chicken. Didn't you hear your mother? . . . But wait till you hear about the surprise I have planned . . ."

Mother stepped back, holding Janie at arm's

reach. “You bide your time, Miss Barry,” she told Tilly.

Then, laying the receiver on the hall table, Mary Chisholm took a firm hold on her daughter and literally propelled her through the front door. It closed behind her with a brisk bang.

Janie was on her way to Sunday School.

CHAPTER TWO

Hi, Lisa

Janie walked down the path to the sidewalk as slowly as she dared. She turned in the direction of the church. Then she stopped and looked around for a rock to kick along. When she found one and sent it flying down the cement, she knew that she was dulling the sheen on the toes of her Sunday shoes. She did not care.

She had known, all along, that she would have to go. She even knew, in her heart of hearts, that she liked going. Miss Andrews, her teacher, was her friend and she knew how to make the lessons come alive. But the fact that Janie liked Sunday School had nothing to do with the fact that the whole thing was unfair. Mother could say what she liked about the others being "too old" but both she and Janie knew that there was a class for boys and girls as old as Rob and Elaine. Now they were in the choir, they claimed they were too busy. But others went to both choir and Sunday School. Mother should have made them.

Janie gave the rock an extra hard kick. It sailed out of sight into a clump of bushes. Janie halted and looked at them. She could go in after it. It would serve everyone right if she got her dress rumpled. But the bushes were full of prickles. She went on walking, leaving the rock behind.

There they all sat, she told herself, scowling fiercely—eating their bacon and talking together and laughing. There Mother stood hearing all about why Tilly had called. And here she was, all by herself, the only Chisholm going to Sunday School.

Maybe Mother had finished on the phone and was even now upstairs discovering Janie's bed unmade.

Janie pulled off her hat with a jerk and swung it in her hand. She'd show them. She shook her head wildly and her fine coppery hair flew every which way, tangling beautifully.

Janie felt better at once. Tilly never wore a hat.

"But, Till, why don't you wear a hat?" Mother had asked Tilly once in Janie's hearing.

"I can't be bothered," Tilly had answered cheerfully.

When I grow up, Janie promised herself, I'll never wear a hat either. And I'll go barefoot. And I'll take my children on a picnic some Sunday morning . . .

What was Tilly plotting? "A surprise," she had said.

Janie came out of her dream world, all at once. She looked around her. The street was perfectly quiet. Everything seemed asleep in the morning sunshine. Even the birds cheeped drowsily. There was not a soul ahead of her on the sidewalk. She *was* going to be late.

Stephanie Jane Chisholm began to run.

She was over halfway when a voice hailed her.

"Janie, how about a ride?"

Gratefully, Janie scrambled into Miss Andrews' car and fought to catch her breath.

"I thought . . . I . . . was going . . . to be late!" she puffed.

"We'll just make it by the skin of our teeth," Miss Andrews said. "I meant to start out earlier but I got involved in a crossword puzzle and I didn't notice the time. What held you up, Janie? You're usually one of the first there."

The dishes, breakfast, arguing with Mother, kicking a rock along, thinking . . . these things could not be told properly.

"My little brother was sick," Janie improvised quickly. "Mother was up with him all night and I didn't want to wake her. So I got breakfast for everybody and I just couldn't get finished in time."

As she spoke, it was very clear in Janie's mind.

She saw herself tiptoeing to her mother's bedroom door, saw her mother fast asleep, her face shadowed with weariness. She pictured herself rounding up Rob and Elaine and whispering orders to them. In her mind, they obeyed her without question, their faces respectful. She was on her way to check on Tim when Miss Andrews brought her back to reality with a bump.

"What's wrong with Tim, Janie?"

Janie searched for something plausible. She hesitated, but Miss Andrews was waiting.

"Measles."

"Measles," Miss Andrews repeated.

Janie sat very still. Tim had had measles at Christmas. Why hadn't she said he had a cold? What would she say when Miss Andrews remembered?

"Let's hope it's a light case of them," Miss Andrews said, parking the car and turning off the motor.

She had not remembered. Janie drew a deep breath. Then the teacher went on, "I guess we won't see your mother in church this morning."

Janie shook her head in mute agreement. Yet not only would Miss Andrews see Mother in church; she might very well see Tim himself going into the Nursery—Tim all scrubbed and shining, without a measle on him.

"I did hear Mother say maybe it wasn't really measles . . ."

Janie heard her own words stumbling wildly. "This morning, his rash was much better or something . . . almost gone. Mother looked at breakfast . . . I mean, after she woke up . . . Just before I left, she woke up and she did look at him then . . ."

She was getting hopelessly lost and she knew it. At last, she stopped and sat silently, waiting for Miss Andrews to ask her, outright, why she had lied.

"Here's a comb, Janie," Miss Andrews said gently instead. "You have about two seconds to subdue that wild mop of hair and get your hat back on. We must look our best because we're being honored with a visit from our celebrity today."

Janie looked through the window. Lisa Daniels was climbing out of her father's car and starting to go into the church. Janie hurried. She and Miss Andrews caught up with Lisa as the three of them entered the Assembly Room.

"Janie!" Lisa cried joyfully, as though she had been waiting for days for that moment to arrive.

Janie smiled shyly.

"Hi," she managed.

Lisa clutched at her elbow and gave it a squeeze. Her blue eyes shone.

"Oh, Janie, I was hoping you'd be here today," she said.

Janie wondered where else she would be on a Sunday morning. It was Lisa, not she, who rarely appeared at Sunday School.

"Girls, take your places. Dr. Howland is waiting," Miss Andrews murmured.

Lisa moved forward to the row of chairs where their class sat but she did not hurry. Lisa Daniels never hurried.

"Hi, Lisa! Hi!" the class chorused as she neared them.

Nobody gave Janie a second glance. Dr. Howland stood at the front, waiting. He cleared his throat crossly.

"I've saved you a seat, Lisa," Marlene Robinson simpered.

The chair beside Marlene was empty, but everyone knew she had not really saved it for Lisa.

"Move over, Marlene," Lisa said coolly. "I want to sit by Janie."

It was like one of Janie's daydreams. She often imagined people saying things like that.

"I want Janie for my team." "Janie is my best friend." "Janie's work is the best in the class." "Janie is the winner again!" "I want to sit by Janie."

It had never happened before. Janie sat down, looking a little dazed.

Dr. Howland read the Call to Worship and announced the first hymn. Pages of hymnbooks rustled. Lisa smiled her enchanting smile and whispered, "I've been hearing things about you, Janie Chisholm."

The piano played the opening chords. Janie, struggling to believe her ears, was saved from having to think of something to say in return as the boys and girls stood up and started to sing.

Janie sang with them but her thoughts were not on the words.

Lisa Daniels was so pretty. She had black, black hair. It was cut short and the ends curled in softly around her face. Summer had only just arrived in Ontario but Lisa was still deeply tanned from the Daniels' winter holiday in Florida. Her eyes, which should have been brown with hair like that, were as blue as a sunny sky. Her smile left you feeling as though you had been given a present.

What could she mean she had been "hearing things"?

"Hey, Janie, would you like me to come over to your house this afternoon?" Lisa offered suddenly. "My parents are away all day . . ."

"Lisa, hush," Miss Andrews warned.

Lisa raised her eyebrows at Janie. Janie still felt she was dreaming the whole thing, but she nodded her head emphatically all the same.

"That would be great," she added, just to make sure Lisa understood.

Lisa turned back to her hymnary. It was settled. Janie, who had lost her place, did not look for it. She simply stood and tried to understand herself.

When Sunday School was over, Lisa did not stay for church.

"See you, Janie," she called over her shoulder as she disappeared.

Janie went to find her family. Tim had already been left in the Nursery.

"Did you meet Miss Andrews on your way in?" Janie wanted to know.

"No. Why?"

"Oh, I just wondered," she said lamely.

Then they were in church and it was too late to ask about Tilly's surprise or to tell Mother about Lisa.

When church was over, Janie still hugged her new secret to herself. She wanted to announce it properly. She wanted to see the whole family startled and impressed. All the way home in the car, she managed not to tell. She would wait until they were at the table.

"Mother, what did Tilly want?" she remembered to ask as they trooped into the house.

Only then did she notice the look on her mother's face.

"I believe you have something to do upstairs in your room before dinner, Janie," Mother said quietly.

Janie reddened.

"I meant . . ."

"Don't tell me what you meant to do." Mother had a note of steel in her voice.

"But if you'd just listen . . ." Janie tried bravely.

"I listened this morning," Mother said. "Now, go."

Janie went.

CHAPTER THREE

Hi, Stephanie

Janie made her bed more carefully than usual. She mitred the corners perfectly and left not even a hint of a wrinkle. Then she picked up some of the clutter and put it away. When she changed out of her church clothes, she even put her dress on a hanger and hung it in the closet where it belonged. When she joined the family for dinner, she felt almost angelic.

When everyone had been served, she could contain herself no longer.

"Guess what?" she burst out. Then, as they looked at her blankly, she realized that there was no way they could guess and she hurried on.

"My friend Lisa is coming over this afternoon."

"What friend Lisa?" Rob asked bluntly. "You don't have any friend called Lisa."

"I do so!"

"This wouldn't be someone you've imagined, would it, Janie?" her father asked.

"The way you imagined you'd made your bed . . ." Mother started.

Then she caught sight of Janie's stricken face.

"I'm sorry, Janie," she said quickly. "Don't look like that. It's just that we've never heard you mention anyone named Lisa before."

Janie swallowed. Her great announcement had gone wrong. They were being horrible, every single one of them.

Elaine saved the day. Her eyes widened.

"You don't mean Lisa Daniels, do you?" she ventured.

"Yes," Janie said simply.

"Are you making it up?"

"Elaine!" Mother said.

She sounded shocked as though she herself had never doubted Janie's word. But Janie was only attending to her sister now.

"I'm not making it up—honest!"

"Lisa Daniels is really coming here to see you this afternoon?"

Janie nodded solemnly.

"Wow!" said Elaine.

It was the moment Janie had been waiting for. Even Dad had heard of Lisa Daniels.

"Isn't she the little girl that comes out of the toothpaste tube?" he checked.

There was a babble of talk as everyone but Tim contributed facts about Lisa and her family.

"That's the one," Mother told Dad. "She's Clare Daniels' daughter."

"Her mother's a model," Elaine breathed. Her face was wistful as she remembered Mrs. Daniels' beautiful clothes in the April *Chatelaine*.

"Her dad's Matt Daniels," Rob added. "He's a disc jockey. He does Matt's Music."

"We know, we know," Elaine said. "And Lisa does TV commercials and models for Eatons' catalog and plays the piano. What I want to know is—since when is she a friend of Janie's?"

Janie retorted too quickly, "We've been friends for ages!"

"Now, Janie," Mother warned.

"Think of a kid Janie's age having all that lovely money!" Rob said dreamily. "What time did you say she was coming?"

"She's coming to see me," Janie stated belligerently.

"Why me?" a voice inside her wondered.

"Me!" Tim yelled joyfully. "Coming see *me!*"

The Chisholms laughed but, under cover of the family uproar, Mother asked again, "What time *do* you expect her, Janie?"

"She didn't say," Janie answered uncertainly.

"This afternoon sometime . . . that's all I know."

When the doorbell actually rang at two-thirty, Janie had to pinch herself to make it seem real.

Lisa swept into the Chisholm house, charming people as she came.

"A baby!" she squealed at the sight of Tim. "You're so lucky, Janie, to have a baby brother—and older brothers and sisters too. It's awful being an only child."

Janie found that hard to credit. She was glad though when Elaine came into the hall.

"Hi, Lisa," Elaine said smoothly when Janie made no attempt to introduce the two girls. "I'm Jane's sister Elaine."

"I was just telling Janie how lucky she was to be one of a big family," Lisa returned. "Being a 'one and only' is a terrible fate."

Elaine and Lisa conversed like equals. Listening to their easy talk, looking at their polite smiles, Janie thought they sounded as though they were both grown-up. Her stomach twisted nervously. Then, she took a deep breath and burst into the conversation, claiming Lisa as her guest.

"Come on up to my room," she ordered gruffly.

Lisa followed obediently.

"Don't you have another brother too?" her voice floated up to Janie, ahead of her on the stairs.

"Two," Janie said absently, wondering how they

could get off the subject of her family. "David's working in Riverside. He's just finished his first year in college."

"What about the other one?" Lisa wanted to know, as Janie opened her bedroom door and stood back to let the other girl go in first.

"The other . . ." Janie was puzzled for a moment. "Oh, my other brother. Rob's fifteen. He's awful!"

"Really?" Lisa was clearly waiting for more.

What else was there to say about Rob? Janie wondered helplessly. He was fifteen, he was her brother and he was awful.

"I guess he's not really so bad," she put in, her loyalty a little late. "He's just like all brothers. Except Tim, of course. And David's okay too when he's home."

Suddenly, overwhelmingly, she missed her brother David. If only he were home to share her excitement over Lisa's coming. David would have known, from the beginning, that Janie was telling the truth about Lisa. The truth came more easily, somehow, when David was there.

"Where is he this afternoon?" Lisa asked idly.

"I told you he's in Riverside . . . oh, you mean Rob," she corrected herself, reading her mistake on Lisa's face. "Who knows? Probably listening to his records. He's always playing his records. He built himself a hi-fi."

"He did!" Lisa was obviously impressed.

But Janie had had enough of Rob. She wanted Lisa to know her, Janie, to like her because she was herself, not because she was part of her family.

She sat very still for an instant, staring at Lisa, trying to make up her mind. Then, clutching at her courage, she began.

"Lisa . . ." Janie's voice was unsteady with excitement—and with fear that Lisa would laugh. Lisa's attention was caught at last.

"What is it?" she asked, as Janie hesitated.

"Lisa, would you call me Stephanie?" Janie begged, all in a rush. "That's my first name, Stephanie, and I've always wanted someone to call me by it but I never told anyone before. I'm so sick of being called Janie. Janie's a baby name, if you ask me."

Lisa almost laughed. Then the intense longing on Janie's face sobered her.

"Sure," she said kindly, speaking in the same voice Mother used when she reassured Tim. "I'll call you Stephanie, if you want. Hi, Stephanie!"

Then she did laugh—and Janie laughed with her. She collapsed onto the bed at Lisa's side. She giggled wildly.

"What sort of records does your brother like, Stephanie?" Lisa asked then.

"All kinds," Janie said, still laughing.

It was wonderful, she thought. She felt different already, like a completely new person.

"I'm Stephanie," she thought proudly. "And Lisa Daniels is my friend."

She had begun to believe it.

CHAPTER FOUR

Janie Belongs

Lisa stayed for supper.

Janie had enjoyed the afternoon. She and Lisa had lain on her bed and talked much of the time. Janie confided her longing for a bicycle, her problems with Elaine, her ideas on how to avoid Sunday School, her admiration of Miss Andrews. This was the way Janie imagined friendship being, having someone to share things with, someone who really listened, someone who cared about important things. Once or twice, Lisa said "Yes" when she should have said "No," and Janie wondered, for a fleeting instant, if the other girl were really listening. But then, Lisa, catching sight of Janie's face, would correct herself swiftly and smile her lovely smile—and Janie would talk on.

Lisa talked too. When Janie pressed her for details about her life as a model and an actress, she gave them. She spoke of her parents, at Janie's insistence. Janie was wide-eyed with wonder when

Lisa announced that her father wrote popular songs.

"He wrote 'A Fistful of Love' and 'Walk Me to the Corner,'" Lisa said. "He composes under a different name and he doesn't talk about it much but he's very good."

"Rob has both those records," Janie breathed. "He just loves 'Walk Me to the Corner.' Wait till I tell him . . ."

Lisa, who had been beginning to sound sleepy, roused suddenly. She wanted to know what other records Rob liked, when his birthday was, whether he went steady with anyone, whether he liked girls.

Janie sighed and told all she knew about her brother Rob. What she did not know, she invented. According to Janie, Rob hated all girls but no less than three of them were fighting over him, tooth and nail. His favorite color was blue, she told Lisa. He wanted to be a pilot when he got out of school.

"My favorite color's blue too," Lisa smiled to herself.

When Janie finally ran out of things to tell about Rob, Lisa went on to question her about David, and then Elaine. When they reached Elaine, Janie balked and suggested they watch television. At five-thirty, Mother came in and asked if Lisa would like to stay for supper.

"I'd be delighted, Mrs. Chisholm," Lisa said prettily. "Could I phone our housekeeper and ask?"

"Your housekeeper?" Mother echoed.

"Yes, my parents are visiting friends in Hamilton and I'm supposed to be spending the day with Mrs. Wallace. I did tell her I was going out but I didn't tell her where I'd be," Lisa said.

Mrs. Wallace was upset when Lisa phoned. From across the room, Janie could hear her voice crackling into Lisa's ear. But Lisa had her way and stayed.

At the supper table, she was the center of attention. Once again, she was questioned about her work. This time, her account sparkled. She told funny little stories about mishaps at the TV studio. She made faces of pretended disgust as she told them all of how she had started modeling when she was a "fat baby" and of how her mother kept a scrapbook of her appearances in magazines.

"She even has one when I was advertising a lotion for diaper rash," Lisa shuddered. "It is horrible!"

Rob roared with laughter. Janie laughed too. Nobody could have helped it. Lisa told it so well, so wittily. Suddenly, studying the enchanted faces of her family, Janie wanted to remind them that this dazzling creature they were enjoying so was her friend, that it was she, Janie, whom Lisa was visiting. But nobody was noticing Janie at all. Even Dad was wholly taken up with the guest.

"Lisa, your supper's getting cold," Mother said all at once. "We're not giving you a chance to eat with our questions. You go ahead and eat right now. And the rest of you, leave her be till she catches up. I have some news for you all anyway, especially Janie."

Lisa gave Mother a measuring glance. Janie had a queer feeling that Lisa did not like being told to eat while Mother talked. But, after a second, she did begin on her meat pie.

"Tilly called this morning," Mother said.

Janie gasped. How could she have forgotten? Questions came from everywhere like a swarm of bees.

"What did she say?" "Is she coming to stay?" "Why didn't you tell us?"

"Matilda Barry is a friend of mine," Mother explained to Lisa. "And she's Janie's godmother."

"She's an artist," Elaine chimed in. "She did those portraits of us behind you."

Lisa swiveled around on her chair and looked where Elaine was pointing.

"She hasn't done Tim yet," Elaine went on. "She's waiting for him to grow old enough to sit still."

"That'll be the day," Rob commented, giving Tim a friendly poke.

"Who's that?" Lisa asked.

Janie stiffened. She had known Lisa would ask. Elaine and Rob were so obviously Elaine and Rob. David's picture was in the living room. That left only one.

"That's Tilly's Janie," Mother said quietly. "Janie was much younger then, of course. I think she was seven, weren't you?"

Janie nodded. She knew what Lisa was thinking. Then Lisa said it.

"I've never seen Janie look like that."

Mother studied the picture in silence as though she were seeing it for the first time all over again. Tilly had drawn Janie sitting by a window looking out over a snowy garden. On the windowsill was a small gray bird, eating daintily. And on the face of the child watching him was a grave beauty, a shining tenderness. It was a very private and special picture.

"Don't talk to me about this one," Tilly had said gruffly when she dumped the big, clumsily wrapped package in Mother's lap. Mother had taken off the wrappings and held up the painting and looked at it. Then, suddenly, without making a sound, she had begun to cry. Janie had never forgotten the strangeness of that moment nor the way Tilly, who rarely kissed anyone, had leaned down and kissed Mary Chisholm on the cheek.

"I have seen her look like that," Mother said now, "but only on rare occasions. I think, though, that Tilly sees her that way nearly all the time."

Janie shied away from the wistful sound in the words and from the open doubt on Lisa's face.

"You still haven't told us what Tilly wanted," Dad said then.

"Oh, yes," Mother remembered. "She's coming for Janie on Saturday morning to take her on an 'expedition.' She wouldn't tell me why or where they would be going. But she did say, if everything worked out, there'd be a surprise for all of us at the finish."

"Maybe she's taking Janie shopping for a birthday present," Elaine suggested.

"Six weeks ahead of time?" Mother was doubtful. "She said not to expect her if it rains. If it's a summery day, she'll be here to pick you up at ten."

"Didn't she invite anyone but Janie?" Elaine asked.

"Who else is there?" Janie said pertly.

She herself had thought of her birthday hopefully, but Mother was right. You wouldn't need to buy a bicycle six weeks early.

Then it was time for Lisa to go. Janie stood watching her get her jacket on. She felt forlorn. The wonderful afternoon was so abruptly over. And tomorrow would be just like all the other days.

"I'll be by in the morning to call for you, Janie," Lisa said. Then she dimpled at the rest of the family. "'Bye, everybody. Good-bye, Rob. I'll be seeing you."

Janie stared after her. Then, coming to her senses, she called, "Sure, Lisa. I'll be ready."

Lisa always came to school with Martha Jefferson and Jo Martin. . . . No, that was before. Lately, she was friends with Pam Potter and Debbie Wellington. Janie checked back in her memory. Yes, Pam and Debbie were the latest. There had been a time when it had been Martha and Jo and a time before that when Suzie Black and Gay Hoffman had always been with her. Always Lisa had been at the center, shining, sure of herself, laughing, and the others had followed along, knowing how lucky they were. Was this the way those friendships had started? Was Lisa really going to walk with her, Janie, in the morning instead of with Debbie and Pam? Janie felt as startled as Alice when she fell into Wonderland. She was just as unsure what would happen next.

When the Chisholms' doorbell rang at eight-thirty, Janie found all three girls on the step, waiting. Debbie and Pam looked uncertain too. Unable to think of a word to say, Janie grabbed her books and joined them.

"I don't think you girls know each other," Lisa

said teasingly as they went down the path to the sidewalk. She was ahead, her arm linked in Debbie's.

Janie, trying to get used to the fact that she was walking to school with three other girls instead of speeding along by herself, did not understand at first. Of course she knew Pam and Debbie. They had never been friends, but all four of them had been in the same class at school all year.

"This is Debbie Wellington and Pam Potter," Lisa introduced them, "And that is Stephanie Chisholm."

Lisa's voice was mocking. Janie gulped, felt foolish, tried to find something clever to say, but remained uncomfortably silent.

"Stephanie," the other two echoed.

"We mustn't call her 'Janie.' It's a 'baby name.'" Lisa quoted Janie's own words.

Janie remembered having said them. They had sounded all right at the time. Now, as Lisa repeated them, they sounded silly even to Janie.

"It *is* a baby name," she defended herself weakly. "And Stephanie is my real first name."

"Stephanie is awfully long." Debbie looked sideways at Janie's troubled face. "I vote we call her Steffy for short."

"Steffy it is," Lisa agreed. Then she leaned close to Debbie and whispered something.

Janie's sharp ears caught the words "How about 'Stuffy'?"

But Lisa was her friend. Janie's hearing must have played a trick on her, she was sure. If Lisa felt that way, why would she have offered to call for Janie? Why had she suggested coming over the afternoon before? It didn't make sense.

"Steffy, what are you making your speech about?" Lisa asked lightly.

Janie looked at her. Lisa glanced back and smiled. Her smile was as gay and friendly as ever.

"Elizabeth Barrett Browning," Janie said slowly. Then, as she thought about it, her voice took on life and sparkle. "She's a poet. David told me about her. Have you ever read this book?"

She held out her library book *The Silver Chord* for them to see.

"David said I'd like it and I did. It's a love story really. Elizabeth Barrett lives in this awful house with her terrible father. . . ."

Janie was off. Lisa barely glanced at the book, but at the magic words "love story," interest kindled in her face.

"So they ran away to Italy." Janie was still talking when they reached the school.

She finished at the classroom door. As the four of them swept into their "home room," Janie was suddenly completely happy, right down to her toes. She was one of them, part of Lisa Daniels' gang, accepted, popular, exciting. She, Janie Chisholm, had arrived.

CHAPTER FIVE

Try Telling the Truth

"Janie, you got some mail this morning," Mother said on Wednesday noon.

Dear Janie,

The surprise is blue, green, gray and gold. It's bigger than a bread-box and smaller than South America.

See you Saturday, love to all, Tilly

Janie read it once and then again. What on earth was blue and green and gray and gold?

"Listen, everybody," she called, and she read Tilly's message aloud.

"She's crazy!" Elaine said. Then she added, honestly, "But I can hardly wait to find out what she's talking about. You're lucky, Janie. Aunt Eileen never takes me on expeditions like that."

"And Tilly never gives Janie clothes or takes her to fashion shows," Mother reminded Elaine. "I think we did pretty well when we chose godparents for you. Rob's the only one who gets neglected. Dick and Susan are so far away in New Zealand that they've forgotten all about him."

"Lisa doesn't have a godmother," Janie said thoughtfully.

"Lisa's mother wasn't an Anglican before she was married, I suspect."

"Lisa says Anglicans are Episcopalians."

"That's what they call them in the United States," Mother agreed. "How did Lisa get to be such an authority?"

"I don't know," Janie said. "We were just talking."

Lisa had made her uncomfortable when they had talked about godparents and Anglicans. But, with Tilly's postcard in her hand, it was hard for Janie to think of Lisa.

". . . Bigger than a bread-box," she mused. "It could be anything."

On Thursday afternoon after school, Janie walked down the hall at a snail's pace. Maybe if she took long enough, Pam Potter would give up waiting and go on without her. Why Lisa bothered with Pam, Janie could not understand. Pam was a heavy-set girl who moved slowly and smiled seldom. Although the two girls had walked to and from school together for four days now, Pam had not yet spoken directly to Janie. When she did say something, she said it to Lisa. And now, Janie was stuck with her.

Janie shouldered open the school door and spotted Pam at once. Neither girl called a greeting. When Janie reached her, though, Pam spoke first.

"Where's Lisa?"

"She and Debbie have to stay in for extra help with their Math. She's furious. She told Mr. Marriott she understood how to do the problems but she was away when we took that new stuff, and Debbie missed half the questions on the test. I said we'd wait for them but Lisa said he takes ages and ages explaining and we should go ahead."

Pam turned and started down the walk. Her shoulders were slumped, her head down. Janie followed.

"I suppose you believed every word of that, didn't you?" Pam said scornfully, all at once.

Janie stopped in her tracks and stared at the other girl.

"Why shouldn't I?" she asked sharply, ready to spring to Lisa's defense.

Pam kept on walking so that Janie had to scurry after her.

"Remember how we exchanged papers and marked each other's after the test," she said. "I marked Debbie's. She got every answer right."

"But Lisa told me . . ." Janie's protest faltered into silence.

Lisa must have told her a lie. Perhaps it had been a mistake, she thought, seeing Lisa's bright face, hearing Lisa's voice saying "Debbie and I are so *mad!*" No, that could not have been a mistake. Janie struggled with the truth, trying to make it fit her picture of Lisa.

"They just didn't want to walk with us, that's all," Pam said dully. "They've done it to me before."

"Maybe they had something private to discuss . . . or something," Janie offered lamely.

How could Lisa! How could she! Janie's thoughts ran around and around in a maddening circle. Which Lisa was real? Why did Lisa bother to lie to her?

"See you tomorrow," Pam said—and Janie realized that they were at her own front door. They had come most of the way in silence.

She repeated "Tomorrow . . ."

"Sure," Pam said, lifelessly. "They'll pick us up tomorrow as though nothing had happened. So long."

Janie trailed into the house.

"How was school?" Mother asked.

Janie scowled. Every day, every single solitary day, her mother asked the same question in the same words.

"Okay, I guess," Janie returned.

Her mother sighed as though she, too, were tired of their daily exchange. But she went on, "Did you walk home with Lisa and the other girls?"

"Yes," Janie told her glibly. "I walked with Lisa really. Debbie and Pam just came along. They're always trying to shove in between me and Lisa but Lisa likes me the best."

"Janie, are you sure that's the way it really is?" her mother questioned.

"Of course I'm sure." Janie felt her cheeks growing hot under her mother's gaze. "Lisa said to me today that they were pests but she's too kind-hearted to drop them. She *did*, Mother. You don't need to look at me like that. You can ask Lisa and see for yourself."

Her stomach gave a sickening lurch as she heard her own last words. But Mother never would ask Lisa.

"Set the table for supper, will you, before you go upstairs," Mother said. "I want to get Tim fed and off to bed. He didn't nap this afternoon and he's as cranky as a bear."

Janie, getting out the knives and forks, tried to

concentrate her thoughts on Tilly's coming and what it meant, on Elizabeth Barrett Browning, on how she missed David, on anything but Lisa's lie and her own. It was impossible. Much as she loved Tilly and David, curious as she was about Tilly's plans for Saturday, interested as she was in Elizabeth Barrett's life, she kept losing her hold on them.

Why? pounded inside her head, over and over again. She was not sure whether it was herself or Lisa she could not understand.

"Janie Chisholm, don't you even know how to set a table properly after all these years?" Elaine's voice cut through the hammering and rescued her. She looked down. Sure enough, the spoons were on the wrong side and she'd given everyone two knives.

She opened her mouth to put Elaine in her place—and then she laughed instead.

"I always eat my soup with two knives," she said.

"And your pie with a spoon, I suppose," Elaine commented. But, to Janie's surprise, she helped straighten out the cutlery and even put on the salt and pepper shakers, which Janie invariably forgot.

She began to sing under her breath as they worked together.

"Walk me to the corner.
Walk me 'round the block.
Walk me to the bus stop

Walk with me and talk.
Walk me to forever
Where we need never part.
Walk me to the corner.
Walk me to your heart."

"You know what," Janie said excitedly, remembering. "Lisa's father wrote that song."

"He did not," Rob said, coming in just in time to catch the last of Elaine's song. "Joey Hallam wrote it."

"He did not!" Janie said hotly. Then she recalled Lisa's exact words and changed her story. "Well, maybe that *is* the name. Lisa said her father used a different name when he wrote music. But he wrote that and another one, too, that you like. I can't remember . . ."

"Look, Stephanie Jane," Rob said, in a patient big brother voice. "You don't have to sell me on Matt Daniels. I think he's great already. And Lisa's an okay little kid. I wouldn't mind having a sister like that instead of the two I'm stuck with. But try telling the truth for once. I saw Joey Hallam play and sing 'Walk Me to the Corner' on TV just last week and he told about how he came to write it. And it *wasn't* Mr. Daniels in disguise either. Honestly, some of the stuff you spout and expect us to swallow! It beats me!"

Janie backed away from him, her eyes snapping with fury. Why, she was telling him the truth. Lisa had said herself .

Lisa . . . Lisa had lied again. Not Janie, Lisa.

"I didn't lie. I'm *not* making up any of it," she began.

But the words which should have burst out of her, sparking with righteous anger, came out weak and unsure, as though she *were* lying.

"Forget it," Rob advised her now. "But, just for a change and a rest, try the truth one of these days and see how you like it."

He went clattering out of the room and up the stairs.

"We're done, Janie," Elaine said. There was a softness in her voice.

She's sorry, Janie thought.

Then she looked at Elaine and understood. Elaine was sorry because she thought Janie had been caught lying. Elaine had not wondered, even for a moment, whether the story might have started with Lisa.

The doorbell rang.

"Janie, there's the paper boy. Pay him, will you?" Mother called.

Janie had to clear her throat before she could call back "Okay," and go to get the money from the kitchen purse.

CHAPTER SIX

Blue and Green and Gray and Gold

"But I still don't know where we're going!" Janie said as she and Tilly, in Tilly's little car, swung into the traffic.

"I know you don't," Tilly laughed. "I thought I'd let the family stew awhile longer. They were so curious it was funny. And I want to see if you and I are as much alike as I think we are."

"How do you mean?" Janie wanted to know.

She curled her feet under her and half-turned to look at her godmother. She felt so comfortable, so at ease with Tilly. She and Tilly fitted together, belonged, just as she and David did. It was a feeling she rarely had with the rest of her family. She did not lie to Tilly.

"Right beside you, on the seat, there's a page out of the newspaper," Tilly explained. "I want you to take it and read it over and tell me, if you were going to investigate one of those ads, which one would it be?"

Janie pounced on the paper and scanned it quickly. It was a page listing SUMMER COTTAGES AND PROPERTIES FOR SALE AND RENT.

"Oh, Tilly, are you going to rent a cottage?"

"Don't ask questions, child. Read," Tilly said sternly.

Janie began at the top and worked her way down. There were cottages with sun decks and boats, cottages with fireplaces and good fishing, cottages with indoor plumbing and easy access to stores. They all sounded wonderful to Janie but no one ad looked special. She read on.

She was in the PROPERTY FOR SALE when she found one.

> FOR SALE: Point with small private
> island. 700′ of shoreline, Call Muskoka . . .

Small private island! There was nothing about fishing or swimming, sun decks or boathouses. Maybe Tilly did not feel the way she did about islands. "Small private island." It sounded like a special place where a girl could go alone and explore and dream and read, perhaps . . .

"Janie, don't just sit there," Tilly laughed. "Tell me what's taken your fancy."

Janie still hesitated. It was such a little ad.

"Janie," Tilly warned. "I'm going to explode."

"Point and small private island . . ." Janie read out slowly.

"That's my girl," said Tilly exultantly. "I knew you'd know a good thing when you saw it. Not that I'm sure it is, mind you. I've marked a couple of others down. We can look at them too. But I want a place where I can take myself and my goddaughter for a holiday. This being a godmother is a serious business, you know. I'm supposed to make sure you're having a proper spiritual upbringing. I think the best way to do it is to take a hand in it myself."

"Oh, Tilly," Janie said. She settled back with a sigh of contentment. She did not even mourn over the bicycle she had pictured so longingly. A point in Muskoka with a small private island!

"Blue and green and gray and gold . . ."

They stopped at the other places first. One looked like a city house transplanted by a lake. It had a patio and a little, neat lawn. Tilly and Janie were scornful when they got back in the car. The other was perched on high rocks. The setting was lovely but the cottage was dingy and cramped. It was painted a mud brown and the two of them left it behind gladly.

Then they were getting close to the point. "THREE MILE LAKE read a sign.

"We must be nearly there," Tilly said. She sounded every bit as excited as Janie.

But first they had to find the man who owned the property. It seemed to Janie to take hours. They finally found his farm. As the little car turned into the lane that wound up to the house, Tilly said, "Janie, remember we may not like it at all. And right now, we must start sounding practical and sensible. Tell yourself it won't be right for us. If it isn't, we'll look again. There are other little islands, I'm sure of that."

Mr. Hollis shook Janie's hand as though she were an adult.

"So you want to see the Point," he smiled at the two of them. "I'll come along and show it to you myself. My wife and I think it's the prettiest point in Muskoka."

Janie tried to act sensible, but her eyes danced and her mouth quirked up at the corners in spite of her. As Hollis went ahead in his car, Tilly reached out her hand and gave Janie's fist an understanding squeeze.

They followed a road which twisted through the Muskoka bush. Silver birches leaned out of the forest of darker trees. Great rocks jutted up on either side of them. Then, suddenly, there would be a glimpse of blue water, a gleaming stretch of lake. Tilly began to sing softly and Janie joined in.

"Land of the silver birch, home of the beaver,
Where still the mighty moose wanders at will,
Blue lake and rocky shore,
I will return once more . . .
Boom-di-di-oom-boom . . ."

The song stopped abruptly as they came over a rise in the dirt road and found themselves perched at the top of a hill so steep the road seemed to fall away from them.

"He said the Point was at the foot of a steep hill," Tilly told Jane unnecessarily, as they inched down.

And there it was to their right.

All her life, Janie was to remember the way the Point looked that first evening when she and Tilly discovered it.

The sun was about to set and the sky was filled with golden light. They climbed out of their cars and just stood. Mr. Hollis felt the same as they did, Janie could tell, for he did not make a sound.

They were standing on top of the ridge which formed the Point. All around them, jack pines soared up into the sky. There was a soft sighing of wind in the trees and a rustle of birds and small animals. It was such a gentle sound it made the silence around them bigger. The golden light, spilling through the tall, tall tree trunks, made

Janie feel as though she were in a church, except that it was lovelier there than at any man-made church she had visited.

Mr. Hollis cleared his throat and said in a voice not much louder than a whisper, "Look around all you like. You can't really see it till you've walked around it. If you've any questions, I'll be glad to answer them."

Tilly took Janie's hand and they started out. Mr. Hollis followed. They found their way down from the high hill to the water's edge. There were a hundred special places there, on the great shelving rocks, where people could lie in the sun or sit and read or have a picnic. They went on further. Janie was holding her breath now. She knew it must be just down here at the tip of the Point, just beyond these trees . . . and then, she saw it.

The island was exactly Janie's size. It was not big enough for a house, but it had a handful of trees, rocks for sitting on, a look of being a separate land, an undiscovered private place. A strip of shallow water, about twenty feet across, separated it from the mainland.

"Oh . . ." Janie breathed.

"Go ahead," Tilly said gently. "Take off your shoes and go on while I talk to Mr. Hollis."

Janie had no word to say. She sat down, pulled off her shoes and socks and stepped into the water.

It was over her knees but not too much. She held her skirt up out of harm's way. She had to go carefully because of the rocks on the bottom. She tried to see them through the water. Then, she found the water growing shallower and she was clambering out onto the rocks.

Tilly had taken Mr. Hollis back the way they had come. Janie could only faintly hear their voices. Then she could not hear them at all. She wandered over the tiny island. It seemed to her as though it knew she was there, as though it was glad she had come at last, as though it had perhaps been there waiting for her for hundreds of years.

She sat down on the top of the biggest rock of all, with her back to the Point. She might have been far out to sea. She could see the far shore, of course, drowsing in a golden haze. But there was no sound of human habitation anywhere.

Whether Tilly bought it or not, whether she, Janie, ever came again, this island would always be hers, put away safely in the secret places in her heart. She wanted to do something, say something, to mark the moment. She thought about it, sitting so still she was like a part of the rock on which she perched. Then, she began to sing, very softly,

"Day is done.
Gone the sun

From the lakes, from the hills, from the sky.
All is well.
Safely rest.
God is nigh."

She had known Taps ever since she was a little girl and Elaine had come home from Explorers singing it. But it had never meant anything out of the ordinary until that moment. The sun had gone now. The air was cooling around her. But still, the sky was touched with light.

She stood up.

"Safely rest," she whispered once more to her own little island.

Then, she left it and started back to find Tilly.

CHAPTER SEVEN

Yippee!

TILLY did not ask: "How was the island?"

She took one look at Janie's rapt face and simply said, "As wonderful as that. Get your shoes on. Mr. Hollis and I have finished our discussion. I'll let you know in the next day or two, Mr. Hollis. Is it all right if Janie and I stay here now and have a picnic before we go?"

"Of course. That's fine," Mr. Hollis said, heartily.

A picnic! Janie's eyes glowed. How did Tilly always know exactly what she was wanting? She had had no idea that Tilly had brought along a picnic. But her godmother produced sandwiches, lemonade and bananas from the back of the car and led the way down to the rocks at the water's edge.

"There's no cottage, Janie. You realize that," she said, as they bit into their first sandwich.

Janie nodded and waited.

"He says there's wonderful fishing . . . but I don't fish," Tilly mused. "There's that shallow place where you waded across. Tim could go in safely there—if we were to buy. And right here, you can dive in. There's room enough for me to paint without having someone breathing down my neck every minute . . . But it costs more than I'd bargained for."

Janie chewed and listened. Tilly laughed.

"You don't say much, do you, miss," she teased. "But you argue better than you know. When I picked you up today, you had such a worried, citified look, as though you were carrying the weight of the world . . . and now, you look as though the world was your Yo-Yo. You're the real, underneath Janie I love."

Janie nearly dropped her sandwich.

"Worried . . ." she echoed.

Then she remembered the moment when Tilly had walked in. Lisa had just called. She had wanted to come over for the afternoon. Janie had told her she was going away.

"Oh well," Lisa had said lightly, "I can always go to Debbie's. But sometimes, she bores me."

Then she had invited Janie to come over to her house overnight next Friday. Janie had felt her heart leap with pleasure at the news that Debbie bored Lisa. But as swift as her pleasure came a sudden hurtful knowledge that Lisa had said such a thing about her friend. And what about the song Lisa had claimed her father wrote? And what about Pam?

"I'd love to come," Janie had said quickly.

But as she hung up the receiver and turned to welcome Tilly, her face had been clouded with small nagging doubts. And Tilly had seen, in that instant, and understood.

"What is the trouble, Janie," Tilly asked now, gently, or is it something you can't talk about?"

"I don't know," Janie said unhappily. "I guess . . . it's Lisa."

Her voice slowed as she spoke Lisa's name.

Tilly held out a banana and listened.

Janie explained who Lisa was. The words did not come easily at first, but soon, she was remembering all of it for Tilly—that morning only a week ago when Lisa had come to Sunday School, the first afternoon, the week of walking to school together, the little things that hurt, Lisa's way of walking first with one and then another, whispering secrets, and, finally, Lisa's lies.

She thought she was done, but then, surprising herself as much as Tilly, she discovered much more to tell. She was always in the wrong at home and she did not know why. Mother, Dad, Rob and Elaine all thought Lisa was so wonderful. And Lisa was wonderful. Janie still thought so—most of the time. But . . . but . . .

"It's the lies she tells," she ended miserably. "I know I tell lies too. But Lisa's . . . I shouldn't mind Lisa's doing it when I do it. I never mean to lie, Tilly. It just seems to happen before I know I'm going to. Lisa's, though, seem different somehow. Worse. But that's awful. Maybe she can't help it either."

Tilly put her banana peelings away carefully before she answered.

"It's such a tangle, Janie," she said at last, speaking thoughtfully. "You're going to have to work it out for yourself. But you should perhaps think about two things. There must be a reason why you tell lies sometimes and why Lisa does too. I think I can guess why you do. You're often a fish out of water at home. You say that yourself. You're younger than the rest, and yet, so much older than Tim. We all want someone to pay attention to us, to see how special and interesting we are. When you're with your parents and Rob and Elaine, I think maybe you feel not special enough and you try to make up a different person you think they'll pay more attention to. Did you ever notice, Janie, that you tell the truth without thinking about it whenever you are with me or with David?"

Janie had known this but she had never stopped to ask herself why.

"David and I talked about it once. I think most of the lies you tell are like 'dress-up clothes.' You try them on to make a different impression. One of these days, Janie, you won't need to deck yourself out in them any longer. You'll discover how interesting the real, true you is, just as she stands. You probably don't believe me—but you will. You'll also come to realize how much easier it is to tell the truth and how fascinating truth can be. Who'd believe you and I would be up here having a picnic on our own point in Muskoka tonight—and yet, here we are. You won't need to make a different story out of it when you get home. It's fun as it is."

Janie nodded. She thought she knew what Tilly meant, but that did not solve the problem of Lisa.

"As for Lisa," Tilly said, as though she could read Janie's mind. "I think her lies *are* different, from what you've said. Maybe Lisa needs to feel her friends depend entirely on her. I don't know Lisa. I'm just guessing. But I'd go carefully if I were you, Janie. Lisa can be cruel, it seems. Try to remember that there are other friends ahead of you. Not that that is any comfort at all, right now, I know."

She got up and looked around her. Evening had come now. It was so still. The sun had dropped and the lake reflected the first stars like a giant mirror. Suddenly, from across the lake, a loon laughed.

"Oh, Janie," Tilly said suddenly, "I love this place already. You and I'll bring a tent until I can get a cottage built. How much longer till school's finished?"

"Three weeks," Janie squeaked, jumping up and staring, wide-eyed, at her godmother's excited face.

"I won't wait till tomorrow," Tilly said, reaching for Janie and giving her a hug. "We'll stop at Mr. Hollis' right now and tell him we must have it."

"Yippee!" Janie yelled, whirling around, tripping on a ledge of rock, and sprawling onto the ground.

"Did you hurt yourself, Janie?" Tilly cried.

Janie did not bother to answer. She just stared up at the great, beautiful sky above her and yelled again, "Yippee!"

CHAPTER EIGHT

Tilly to the Rescue

"I THINK, perhaps, I won't come in, Janie," Tilly said, as she halted the little car in front of the Chisholms' house. "It *is* getting late and I have to get back to North York tonight. Besides, I'd like you to have the fun of telling them yourself."

"No, Tilly," Janie's voice rose in alarm. She clutched at her godmother's arm. "You have to come in and tell them. They won't believe just me."

Tilly looked down at the earnest face beside her. Her lips set suddenly.

"Oh, they won't, won't they," she said grimly. Then she patted Janie's hand and went on in her ordinary voice. "Well, I didn't want to leave anyway. I'm dying to see your parents' faces when they hear what mad Matilda Barry has done now. Move, Janie."

Janie scrambled out of the car and ran for the house.

"Here they are!" Mother called, to the rest, meeting them in the hall. Chisholms assembled from all directions. Only Tim, asleep in his crib, was missing. Their eyes were fixed on Tilly's face. Tilly simply smiled at them and led the way to the living room. The questions were flying long before they had each found a chair. Janie, for greater safety and support, sat cross-legged on the floor at her godmother's feet.

"Tell us, Tilly. We've been dying of curiosity all day," Mother said.

"What did you take Janie for?" Elaine wanted to know, envy plain in her voice. "Was it something for her?"

"They probably just had a picnic," Dad guessed, looking at their empty hands.

"Picnic nothing," Rob jeered. "Look at their faces. They look like . . . like . . ."

"Like Tim when he's been into my cupboards while my back was turned," Mother laughed. "Till, don't be so mean. Tell us."

"Why ask me?" Tilly countered. "Janie was there. She can tell you the whole story."

"Let's not have Janie's version," Rob answered, only half-teasing. "I'd like to know what really happened."

"Rob, hush," Mother told him. She turned to Janie then.

"What happened, dear?" she said.

Janie savored her importance for one long, silent moment. They were all just sitting there, watching her, waiting for her to speak.

"Tilly bought an island!" she burst out then, "and a point," she added.

There was an immediate uproar.

"An island! Where?"

"A point . . . land? Oh Till, you didn't . . . did you?"

"Where? You mean, a real island . . . a body of land entirely surrounded by water?" Rob wanted to be sure.

"Go on, Janie. Tell them the whole story," Tilly said quietly.

They were on the edges of their chairs now but they hushed finally and waited for more.

Janie started at the beginning. As she told, step by step, of the wonderful day, she remembered Tilly telling her how "fascinating" the truth could be. Tilly had been right. She, Janie, did not need to add to the truth this time. It was perfect just as it had really happened.

But the other Chisholms kept interrupting. Over and over, they asked "Did you really, Tilly?" "Is that true, Tilly?"

When Janie told about the two of them going back to see Mr. Hollis and recounted the way Tilly had announced, "I'll buy your point and island, Mr. Hollis. I'm not sure where the money will come from but I'll find it. My goddaughter needs that island for personal and private reasons and I intend she should have it." Even Mother was doubtful.

"Till, what did you really tell the man?" she said "Janie's story is all very well, fantastic in fact, but what actually went on?"

"We know our Janie too well, I'm afraid," Dad backed Mother up. He smiled at Janie as he said it but he continued. "She likes to embroider the truth. We count on her to entertain us. But this time we want the facts . . . You understand, don't you, Janie?"

Janie stared at her parents. She was telling the truth. She had not said one untrue word. A sob pushed up into her throat suddenly, and she could not manage speech. She swallowed desperately and tried to understand what was happening to her.

Then Tilly exploded.

"It so happens," she said, her tone icy, "that Janie has not lied. She has not even exaggerated. She has remembered details I would not have thought of and has told you about our afternoon better than I could have. Yet, from the moment we arrived, from the moment we stepped inside that door, every one of you has been expecting her to lie. Every one of you has been sure, positive, absolutely certain, you could not trust this child. If I were Janie, I'd lie too. Or I just would not ever tell any of you anything. I suppose Rob and Elaine have told the truth, the whole truth and nothing but the truth all their lives. That is something *I* don't believe! As for you, Mary, I can remember more than once when you . . . shall we say . . .'dramatized' the truth a bit? Oh, the lot of you make me sick and tired."

Tilly was on her feet, by this time, heading across the room.

"I *did* buy a point and a tiny island in Muskoka," she hurled back at them over her shoulder. "And I was planning to have the lot of you up to visit me this summer. Now I'm not so sure I want you. Janie and I have no trouble believing in each other. I wouldn't want you doubting my word every time I turned around."

"Till, don't be ridiculous," Mother finally managed to stem the flood of words.

She and Dad were in the hall now, with Tilly. Rob, Elaine and Janie sat where they were. None of them looked at each other.

"Heavens, Matilda, what an outburst," Dad said. He sounded embarrassed.

Then, Janie was stunned to hear her mother say slowly and painfully, "I . . . maybe you're right, Tilly. I see what you mean, although I didn't notice it before. You always have understood Janie better than I. Rob and Elaine . . ."

Dad shut the door. The three children could hear only a murmur of voices now. They still sat, not one of them knowing what to do or say.

Janie was dazed. Tilly had gone into battle for her, like a knight riding into a tournament. It had been wonderful, for a moment, but frightening too. Now, as she strained her ears to hear what was being said in the hall, she saw with a flash of insight that Tilly had been only partly right. Mother had told her, Janie, over and over again that nobody trusts a liar. She thought of her own way of weighing everything Lisa said, testing for flaws, looking for what did not fit, ever since she had discovered that Lisa lied. She was Lisa's friend—but she knew better than to believe Lisa without question. She, herself, had made her family distrust her. If she wanted them to take what she said on faith, she would have to stick to what was true until she had earned their trust.

It was a difficult thought. She would not have been able to work it out except that Mother had explained it to her so often. She had not listened—but she had heard.

"Hey, you guys," she said. Her voice seemed to thunder in the silence but she went on bravely. "You wait till you see Tilly's place. There's a marvelous rock you can dive right off and, Rob, Mr. Hollis told us there's terrific fishing."

"We may never get there," Elaine said in a growl.

Then, startling the three of them, came a burst of laughter from the hallway. The three adults were having fun together, not fighting any longer.

"Oh yes, you will," Janie smiled. "You'll see."

CHAPTER NINE

Steffy Catches On

Janie gobbled her breakfast with the speed of light on Monday morning. She could scarcely contain herself. Wait till the other girls heard about her own private island. Well, Tilly's island really—but Tilly herself had said that she was getting it for Janie.

She was on the step watching for the others five minutes before they appeared. As they came down the sidewalk, Rob wheeled his bicycle out of the garage. Lisa darted away from Debbie and Pam.

"Hi, Rob," she breathed, popping up right in front of him so that he had to stop for a moment if only to navigate around her.

"Hello," Rob grinned down at her pixy face.

"How about offering a girl a ride on your handlebars?" Lisa suggested.

"One girl I might be able to handle, but four, no thanks!" Rob answered, turning the wheel and starting around her.

Lisa shifted so that she again blocked his path.

"I don't mean *them,*" she said scornfully, jerking her shoulder at Janie, Debbie and Pam who stood in a row, watching. "They need the exercise. How about taking just me?"

Rob laughed. "Ask me again in five years, Lisa, and you might have yourself a date," he told her.

With a quick move, he maneuvered the bike past her, swung himself onto it and sped away down the road toward the high school.

Lisa simply stood where she was, gazing after him, her eyes shining.

"You'd think she'd catch on that, to him, she's just a little kid," Pam made a low comment.

Janie's eyes widened and both Pam and Debbie laughed. Lisa had still not joined them. Debbie summed it up.

"You'd think Steffy would catch on that, to our Lisa, she's just Rob's kid sister," she taunted.

So that was what Lisa had meant on that first day when she said, "I've been hearing things about you, Jane Chisholm." She must have only lately discovered that Rob and Janie were related. No wonder she was forever asking questions about him, his taste in records, his favorite color. Janie should have felt wounded but she could not. It was too funny. The thought of anyone thinking Rob was something special ticked her and she giggled.

Pam joined her and, belatedly, Debbie.

"What's so funny?" Lisa came quickly to where they waited.

"It's Steffy," Debbie answered. "She's being silly, that's all."

Suddenly, Lisa remembered what Janie had told them about Tilly's mysterious "expedition."

"What did that woman want?" she questioned, as she went ahead, with Pam today. "Did she give you a present or anything?"

Janie spilled out the whole story.

"She sounds crazy," Lisa said when Janie told about the ad in the paper. "Is she rich?"

"Rich? Tilly? Heavens, no! She's an artist. She lectures at the University on art, too, but she's certainly not rich."

Lisa looked disappointed. Janie went on. When she got to the part about the island, she saw a new Pam. The girl who had seemed dull and lackluster to Janie had turned and was walking backwards so that she would not miss a word. Her face was bright with wonder and astonishment, as though she had been with Janie in those few moments on the little island. Janie could not tell them about singing Taps out there. Lisa and Debbie would have laughed at her. But, sometime, when she and Pam were by themselves, she might be able to share it with her.

"You mean to say there's no cottage at all?" Lisa asked.

"None," Janie said happily. "We're going to live in a tent this summer, Tilly says, and she's going to have a little cabin built maybe. Just one room. 'Just enough roof to get in under when it rains,' she said."

"Is there a boat?" Debbie wanted to know.

Janie shook her head.

"A dock?"

"No."

"A raft or diving board?"

"No, of course not. I told you—just land."

"Heavens," Lisa said dryly, "and you sounded all excited! Why, there'd be absolutely nothing to do in a place like that. Is there a town close by?"

"I think Tilly said the nearest one is four or five miles away." Janie tried to be accurate.

Somehow, as they talked, Debbie and Pam had changed places. Debbie and Lisa were clearly in complete agreement over Tilly's property.

"I can't see what you're all steamed up about, Steffy." Debbie made a face. "My parents want to go to our cottage for a month and I'm begging them to let me stay in town with my aunt. There's no TV there, no shows, nobody to talk to but the family, nowhere to go."

"No boys!" Lisa put in, and she and Debbie laughed.

Janie thought of the Point—of all the picnic places, of the swimming she would do, of the rocks where she could curl up with her book, of the woods to explore.

She tried to keep her face blank so that Lisa and Debbie would not see there how she pitied them.

"Oh, Janie, you're so lucky," Pam murmured.

Janie nodded. "I know," she said simply.

CHAPTER TEN

At Lisa's

All week, Janie waited for Lisa to mention the fact that she had invited Janie to spend the night at her house on Friday. Lisa had suggested Monday first, but Mother had refused to let Janie go visiting on a school night. The days passed. Lisa did not refer to it.

Janie tried to bring herself to say, "I'm looking forward to Friday night." She would get the words ready. She would have them right on the tip of her tongue. But, somehow or other, they were never spoken.

Debbie and Pam were always with the other two. Perhaps that was why Lisa did not say anything. Perhaps she was being tactful. Janie, knowing Lisa better by now, did not honestly think that tact would keep Lisa quiet, although she could not find any other explanation.

When Friday itself arrived, Janie was decidedly uneasy. Suppose Lisa had forgotten! The Chisholms were expecting Janie to go. Dad was going to drive her over after supper. Mother had even bought her new pajamas to wear, gay shortie ones with ruffles across the seat.

Finally, in the afternoon as they were going from Art to Music, Janie did manage to go hurriedly, almost under her breath, "I'll see you after supper, Lisa."

"Huh?" Lisa responded. Then, an expression Janie could not fathom crossed her face. "Oh . . . sure, Steffy," she said lightly, brushing past and preceding Janie into the classroom.

Janie did not try again but, inside her, a guard went up. Whatever happened, she was prepared.

The family made much over her as they helped her pack. Ever since Tilly's surprising outburst, the Chisholms had been trying harder to make Janie feel their love and concern. As Elaine came in to offer her silver-backed comb and brush set; as Rob called up, "Are you ever lucky to be visiting Matt Daniels! Let me know if he wants to hear some teen-age talent, won't you?"; as Mother helped her pack and Tim thoughtfully unpacked everything Mother had so carefully arranged in the suitcase, Janie groaned to herself. They were trying so hard. They were being so nice. They imagined that they were doing what Tilly would have done, behaving toward her as David did. Janie knew, in that moment, Tilly and David would have seen that she was worried about going to Lisa's. Tilly and David would have stopped getting ready long enough to find out what had gone wrong. But the others did love her—and she loved them.

"Thanks a lot, Elaine," she said, handling the comb and brush reverently.

"Okay, I'll get you an audition," she yelled back at Rob.

"That's perfect, Mom," she told her Mother—and then, they both laughed at Tim and his helpful ways.

It seemed only seconds later that she and Dad were pulling up in front of the Fairview Apartment where the Danielses lived.

"Shall I just drop you here, Janie?" Dad asked. "I guess you know your way, don't you."

"No . . . please, wait for me, Daddy." Janie slipped into the childish name without thinking. She added, still not getting out of the car, "I've never been here before."

Then, her father astonished her by saying, just as Tilly would have, "Why don't I walk up with you? I'd like to see inside and we might as well make sure she's really expecting you."

Janie was too grateful for speech. They went together into the lobby. Dad found the right button and pushed it. A voice came through a speaker in the wall.

"Who is it?"

"Jim Chisholm," Dad said, his voice strong and sure.

"Oh . . ." the woman sounded startled. "Okay. I'll buzz for the door to open."

"Heavens," Dad said mildly, as the buzzer sounded, the door clicked and he and Janie pushed through it into the long, carpeted hall. "What a place for a child!"

Janie was not sure what he meant but she was glad she was not Lisa. It was so hushed, so rich-looking, so dead. Nobody would ever, ever dare to run or sing in a place like this.

The elevator slid them silently to the fourteenth floor. The Daniels' apartment was down the hall to the right. A lady was standing at the door. This was not Lisa's mother, Janie knew. She was much too roundabout and elderly to be a model.

"Yes, Mr. Chisholm, what can I do for you?" she asked pleasantly.

Janie just stood. Dad explained. The lady looked distressed.

"I'm so sorry, darling," she said, peering down at Janie.

Janie winced at the endearment.

"Lisa's gone to the theater with her parents and Debbie . . . Debbie . . ."

"Wellington," Janie supplied automatically.

"I think that *is* the name," the lady agreed. "She must have completely forgotten you were coming for she never once mentioned it. I keep house for Mrs. Daniels and I would have known if Lisa'd been expecting anyone. I see that things are ready. Are you sure you didn't get the dates mixed up, honey? Perhaps it was next weekend . . ."

"But . . ." began Janie. The words stuck in her throat. She looked up at her father.

"I'm sure there's been some such mistake, Mrs. . . ."

"Wallace," the lady supplied.

"Wallace," Dad echoed, his hand cupping around Janie's shoulder and squeezing comfortingly. "Would you mind not mentioning this to Lisa when she comes home? Janie would rather Lisa didn't know she got mixed up about it, wouldn't you, Janie?"

"Yes," Janie said.

Mrs. Wallace assured them she would never say a word. She was going on about the Daniels family when Dad, politely but firmly, withdrew himself and his daughter from the doorway and escaped to the elevator.

All the way down, Janie's heart grew heavier and heavier. She did not mind not staying, but Dad must think she had made up the whole thing, invitation and all.

They were in the car. The car was on its way home. Then Dad spoke.

"That was a cruel thing Lisa did, Janie," he said.

"Lisa did!" Janie's heart leapt.

"But, Dad, you said I'd got it 'mixed up,'" she quoted him.

"Suppose Lisa did forget. I can see you think she did not and I suspect you are right, but let's suppose, for a moment, that she honestly forgot. It would make her feel badly to learn that you had come and found her not home, wouldn't it?"

"Sure," Janie said, following him, but unconvinced about Lisa's innocence.

"Now, let's suppose, instead, that she did it on purpose. Maybe she didn't mean to, at first, but then, when her parents arranged this theater trip, suppose Lisa deliberately let you think you could still come and spend the night with her. We all have a mean streak, Janie. Maybe Lisa has a bigger one than some, but we all have one. Think how powerful she'd feel when she came home and discovered you'd actually taken her at her word and come—and found she'd gone."

"Oh," Janie said slowly. She was beginning to see.

"Mrs. Wallace has promised not to tell her. I think we can trust her though I would not be surprised if that woman loves to talk. But she *did* promise. Now, Janie, if were you, I wouldn't say a word."

"Let Lisa wonder, you mean," Janie filled in. "Not say anything at all?"

"Not a word," Dad said solemnly. "If she forgot, it is the kind thing to do. If she didn't forget, it . . ."

"It will serve her right," said Janie. The car had come to a stop. Her father was waiting for her to get out and go on in. They were certainly going to be surprised to see her back so soon, Janie thought. She leaned over her suitcase, bulky on the seat between them, and gave her father a quick, almost shy kiss.

"Thanks, Dad," she said.

"Think nothing of it," Dad grinned at her. "It's all part of being a parent. One gets used to the unexpected. Now, away you go and tell the others."

Relief suddenly rose in Janie like bubbles in new ginger-ale. She bounced out of the car and flew up the walk. She did not have to go to Lisa's. She could sleep in her own bed! And she still had the new pajamas!!!

CHAPTER ELEVEN

"Your Brother's Home!"

Nobody but Tim noticed Janie's joyous entrance.

"Janie! Janie!" he yelled and threw himself at her knees.

Janie was not flattered. He went through the same performance every afternoon when each of them came in from school. But she was glad to see him. She scooped him up and hugged him till he squeaked. He was laughing uproariously at her when Mother appeared to see who was making the commotion.

"Janie!" she cried. The delight in her voice was so like Tim's that Janie was startled. She had left only half an hour ago. Mother should have been astonished to see her—but she looked excited instead.

"I'm so glad to see you, though I've no idea why you're here," she said, sounding as scatterbrained as Janie had ever heard her. "Your brother's home."

Janie stared at her. Then the meaning of the words dawned on her.

"David!"

"Yes, he's in the living room. Go on in and . . ."

But Janie did not wait to be told. Dropping Tim, she raced for the living room door. David, hearing her voice, came hurrying to find her. Crash! They collided head-on. Janie gasped for air and went to stand back and give David room to breathe. David, however, was not interested in breathing. He crushed his younger sister in a bear hug, until she squealed for mercy just as Tim had done earlier.

"They told me you were out for the evening," he said, when, at last, he let her go.

"Yes, Janie. Why aren't you at Lisa's?" Elaine said suddenly.

"I think Lisa did a neat double-cross," Dad explained, grinning a welcome at his tall son, even as he started to tell the others about Lisa's not being there.

Janie's eyes searched every face, watching for the "This is one of Janie's stories" look. But nobody was doubting her. They were angry. Even Mother, who was forever reminding them that people "meant well," looked as though she would like to get her hands on Lisa Daniels. Rob spoke up suddenly.

"I wasn't going to tell you because I thought the

kid was such a friend of yours, Janie," he said, "but she's an awful pill of a kid, if you ask me. She actually was waiting for me outside the school the other day when I came out after my exam. There I am, with a whole bunch of guys, and here's this ten-year-old kid yelling 'Rob! Rob!'"

He called his own name in a falsetto imitation of Lisa, and Janie doubled over with laughter. Through her giggles, she did straighten him out though. "She's not ten. She's twelve!"

"Ten . . . twelve, what's the difference! She's still an infant in arms!"

"Expecially when you're all of fifteen yourself!" David teased.

"Aw, cut it out!" Rob growled, aiming a poke at his brother.

"Go on, Rob. What happened?" Elaine begged.

"Well, she kept on like that and the others said, 'Who's your friend, Robert?' and stuff like that. Rocky Jamieson said, 'Aren't you going to speak to the little lady, Rob? We'll chaperone.' Well . . ."

"Stop saying 'well' all the time—but go on," Mother urged, annoyed with herself for interrupting him.

"Well . . . I mean . . . I said, 'What do you want, kid?' I thought maybe Janie needed something. Heck, I didn't know what. But she looks at me all gooey-like and she says, 'I'm late getting home,

Rob. Would you mind riding me home on your crossbar?'"

"So did you?" Dad said. His eyes twinkled.

"Are you kidding?" Rob yelped. "I just told her the truth. The whole brutal truth. I said, 'Look, kid, I'm too big to play with little girls. And you don't happen to live out my way. You're ten years too young for me,' I told her, 'and going the way you're going, add ten years on and I still wouldn't be interested.'"

David whistled. Dad shook his head over Rob's gentlemanly behavior. Mother laughed. Elaine applauded. Janie stood very still, feeling suddenly sorry for Lisa.

"So that's why no Lisa was there tonight," Dad said slowly. "She was taking revenge. Janie was the logical one to lash out at. I think, Janie, that you'd better be *sure* not to mention this to Lisa."

"Don't worry," Janie said earnestly. "I wouldn't know what to say. But I wish I didn't have to walk with her on Monday. Maybe, if I called Pam . . ."

"Jim, I think now might be the time," Mother said.

"Time for what?" Dad looked at her blankly.

Janie, still worrying about Monday morning, was not paying much attention. Calling Pam would not solve things. She would just have to explain. She was almost sure Pam would understand. But

Pam might tell. And even if she did not, she and Janie would still have to walk with Lisa and Debbie, as always, or Lisa *would* know her revenge had worked.

"Oh, Jim, really!" sighed Mother. "Remember what brought David here tonight."

Why had David come? Janie began to listen. David had a job working in Riverside, this summer, for Andrew Copeland. He was doing construction work and getting hard muscles and a deep, deep tan doing it. But he had not been coming home for weekends. It was too far to come and, besides, he was dating Sally Copeland.

"Oh . . . of course," Dad said. "I'd forgotten just for the minute. Rob's gallant way with women put it out of my head."

Rob blushed and they all laughed.

"But I agree," Dad said then. "No time like the present. A pun, Mary! No time like the 'present' . . ."

"Really!" Mother said again, disgusted with him. She had no patience with his puns. All the children were punsters too. And, according to Mother, she had yet to hear any of them, children or father, make one really good one.

Now she turned to Janie who was on the verge of asking what on earth they were talking about.

"Janie," she said, smiling a special smile that made Janie's heart begin to thump. Something was about to happen. "You *do* remember what is going to happen here on July seventeenth, don't you?"

"My birthday," Janie replied, her eyes popping.

"Well," Mother began.

Rob could not resist. "I do wish you wouldn't say 'well' all the time, Mother," he scolded her.

"What?" she said, startled, stopping what she was saying. Janie wanted to shriek. She controlled herself with iron will power.

"Mother!" she begged.

"Don't you interrupt me again, Robert, whatever I say!" Mother commanded. "Oh Janie, I'm sorry. Well . . . I mean, David has brought your present, from your father and me, here from Riverside. It's secondhand. He found out they wanted to sell it and asked for it. Meg Copeland's too big for it now, but I'm sure it will be just right for you. And your father agreed. So, instead of waiting till your birthday . . ."

"Mary, for goodness sake, her birthday is going to come and go while you stand and talk." Dad halted the flood of words. "Go on out and bring it in, David."

David, who had been waiting too, dashed out to the garage. Elaine was jigging up and down by now, not at all like a sedate fourteen-year-old.

"Oh, Janie, just wait till you see!" she sang at her sister.

"David gone?" Tim said in a worried voice.

"He's coming back, darling," Mother told him, but she never took her eyes off Janie's face. Thus, she caught the blaze of glory there when David struggled through the doorway and placed, squarely in front of his sister, the bicycle of her dreams.

Janie stared at it, her mouth agape, looked around at the beaming circle of faces, tried to speak, made a croaking noise instead, and then, grabbed Tim to her and hugged him all over again. He was not too surprised. He was used to being loved by his family.

"Janie, Janie," he said tenderly, patting her cheek with his pudgy hand.

And Janie promptly, wetly and happily, burst into tears.

CHAPTER TWELVE

Pam

Janie heard the kitchen clock strike one that night. She was too happy, too strung up with excitement, to sleep. She lay awake, not minding a bit, and dreamed of riding her bicycle. She pictured Meg Copeland riding it. David had told them about Meg. She had ginger hair like Janie's own and she was a family rebel, too, except that she was the baby of her family. She was in high school now and was becoming quite a tennis player, according to David. Her bike had not been used in the last couple of years. High school girls, in Riverside, did not ride bicycles.

"They must be crazy," Janie told herself. But she thought gratefully of Meg, all the same. Dad knew Mr. Copeland. They had gone to school together. And David talked of the family as though he had been friends with them for years rather than just a few weeks. Maybe, someday, Janie would meet Meg.

Her thoughts left Meg and returned to the bicycle. It had been painted and repaired. It had a brand-new bell, David's present, and a basket hung on its handlebars. Meg had used that. Janie imagined herself riding, winging free and wild as the wind, swooping up one street and down another, her hair blowing back, her cheeks cooled by the breeze she herself was making.

It could not possibly be as wonderful as her imagination made it. Yet, when she actually climbed onto the bike and sailed away down the street, she discovered that it was better. The real thing was so much more . . . real. She sped along, pedaling furiously, coasting down hills, getting off and pushing up them a couple of times. And it was so perfect that she could scarcely believe it.

All weekend, she rode her bicycle. Sunday School stopped her for an hour, church for another. But she did not waste time arguing. She was using every last minute to ride and then looking forward to the moment when she would be free to ride again.

"I'll forget what you look like," Mother warned her.

Janie only laughed.

Lisa was not at Sunday School. Janie had wondered if she might be and had readied herself to face her there. She was relieved when Lisa did not show up. Miss Andrews noticed a difference in Janie the moment she saw her.

"What's happened to set you aglow?" she asked.

"I have a new bicycle," Janie told her.

"Oh, Janie, how lovely. I know how you've longed for one. Is it everything you dreamed it would be?" Miss Andrews asked, smiling.

Janie nodded. "Everything," she said.

She almost forgot to telephone Lisa to tell her not to call for her in the morning. She remembered as she came into the house after racing around the park three times on the bike.

"Hello," Lisa answered the phone herself.

"Hi, Lisa," Janie panted into her ear. "This is me, Janie."

"Janie," Lisa's voice sharpened. Then she drawled slowly, "What's the matter?"

"Nothing, nothing at all," Janie told her gaily. "I just called to tell you not to bother picking me up tomorrow. I have a new bike. I'll be riding to school from now on."

"A what?" Lisa could not believe her ears.

"A bicycle," Janie said plainly. " 'Bye, Lisa."

"My mother says they're dangerous!" Lisa shrilled before Janie could hang up.

"My mother doesn't," Janie said sweetly.

Click. The receiver was back in place. She had done it.

Janie reached school first on Monday. With nearly half an hour to spare, she got involved with the people in a book. When Lisa, Debbie and Pam came in, carried along on a wave of Lisa's bright chatter, Janie did not even notice them for a moment. Portia and Julian, in Elizabeth Enright's *Gone-away Lake*, were taking her whole attention.

Lisa would have ignored her in return. Perhaps, even if Janie had spoken, Lisa would have passed her by. Neither of them was quite sure what she should do. But Pam had other ideas.

"Janie, have you really, truly got a bike?" she demanded.

"Yup!" Janie said, laconically. Her eyes were gleaming with pride, though. Pam was not fooled.

"Oh, everything nice happens to you!" she said.

Janie had been happy clear through, but Pam's words came as a shock. She had known she was lucky. She was delighted with her bike. But she had been a misfit for so long that she was used to feeling slightly sorry for herself. Pam's eyes, dark with envy, left no room inside Janie for self-pity.

"Nice things happen to you too," she said lamely.

"Name one," Pam countered.

"Pam, that was the bell," Lisa hissed. Pam scuttled to her desk. It was time to begin being enriched.

Janie only half-liked "enrichment" days. She and her friends were all in the "bright" class. Very few of them had any examinations to write. Instead, they saw films, heard speakers, went on field trips. But always, in the back of Janie's mind, were the other boys and girls in the school. She could feel them, see them almost, scowling anxiously at the examination questions, chewing the ends of pencils, wondering whether or not they would pass. Elaine had been such a student. She still had to work very hard and get extra help to make average grades. Janie had often heard her bitter comments on "the smart kids" and their "smugness." Janie never had a defense ready when Elaine began. She knew that many of her classmates were smug. She knew that she, herself, would never think of telling the rest her guilty feelings about being "enriched."

"Who needs to be enriched the most?" Elaine would ask.

Her argument made sense to Janie. Maybe, if Elaine had been allowed to see films like this one, she would have become excited about Math. Maybe. Janie shook her mind free and tried to get excited herself.

They had recess that day. Now that they were in junior high, recess was usually a thing of the past. Janie felt like a little girl again as the class swarmed out onto the playground. The others must have shared her feelings this time, for in less than a minute some were playing tag, some hopscotch on the squares painted for the Primary children, and one giggling group was circling around playing London Bridge.

Janie was content to watch. It was hot. The sky was as blue as a sky could be. It made her eyes ache to look up at it for more than an instant. She leaned against the wall, luxuriating in just plain dreaming of nothing in particular. Pam joined her quietly, leaned with her, perhaps even dreamed the same dream.

"You two look like a couple of cows," Lisa said fretfully, breaking out of the lineup for London Bridge and coming over to stand in front of them. Janie blinked lazily at her. It was a good description. Right at that moment, she felt as contented, as placid as a cow.

"Nice cows," she said drowsily. "Aren't we, Pam?"

Pam laughed deep in her throat. She sounded as though she were laughing in her sleep.

"Oh, honestly," Lisa stamped her foot at them. "Where's the new bicycle?"

Janie came awake at that. Her eyelids, heavy with sunshine and laziness, flew up. She smiled broadly at Lisa, her friend after all.

"Over in the bike stand. Come on and I'll show

you," she offered, shoving herself out from the wall and starting off.

Lisa smiled, a small satisfied smile.

"No, thanks, Stuffy," she said clearly. "I've seen plenty of bikes before. I'm sure yours is nothing special. I just wanted to know if you really had one or were only telling one of your usual lies."

She turned on her heel, leaving Janie staring after her. Over her shoulder, she tossed back, "Coming, Pam?"

"Not right now," Pam answered.

"Suit yourself," Lisa said, her back still turned. Then she was back in the game, playing as noisily as anyone there, paying no attention to the two by the wall.

"She wanted you to say that," Pam commented.

"I know," Janie said dully.

The morning no longer seemed to shine. There was something hurtful about the way Lisa had walked away. Janie tried to put it out of her mind. She had finished with Lisa already. Lisa was not her friend, had not been her friend ever, really. Lisa had wanted Rob to notice her, that was all. Janie reminded herself of these facts. There was no arguing with any of them. Lisa had lied to her. Lisa had hurt her on purpose. Lisa had a mean streak, all right, as Dad had said—except Lisa's mean streak ran right through her.

"She feels bad," Pam said slowly, her thoughts following Janie's.

"I know," Janie said again. She did not know how she knew. She was not even sure she and Pam were right. But there had been a lost look to Lisa's shoulders as she walked away from them, a hunched-up look, as though she felt alone now that they had deserted her.

"Only *she's* the one who did it to herself," Janie protested, through Pam had not spoken in Lisa's defense.

This time it was Pam who said, "I know."

They leaned again, not really contented this time, just two girls waiting for the bell to call them back to class.

"Tell me about your point and island again," asked Pam, after a couple of moments of silence.

Happiness flowed back into Janie like a golden river. Words spilled out of her. This time, softly so that no one else would catch a word of it, she did tell Pam about her first trip out to the tiny island, about singing Taps to it, about the silence there and the stars. "And in just two weeks, Tilly and I will be there!" she finished exultantly.

Pam's sigh brought her back to earth.

"What do you do in the summers, Pam?" she asked, more out of politeness than curiosity.

"I stay right here most of the time," Pam said

dully. "My aunt gets only a two-week holiday and she takes it in the fall. She goes out West to visit my other aunt and I stay with my grandmother then. We go for drives on weekends sometimes, but my aunt doesn't like cottages. She says it's more comfortable right at home. I guess, for her, it is. She has arthritis and . . . well, anyway, that's what I do."

Janie remembered now. Pam's parents had been killed when the bus they were riding on had collided with a train. It had happened years before, when Pam was only two or three. Pam's aunt worked in a dry goods store downtown. Before that, it seemed to Janie, she had worked for Lisa's mother. She had had something to do with Lisa's mother anyway. Someone had guessed once that Lisa put up with Pam because their families were friends . . . or something. It was vague in Janie's mind. When she had heard it, she had not known she and Pam would ever be friends.

"Friends," she thought wonderingly. "I suppose we are. Not Lisa and me . . . Pam and me."

"I'm sorry, Pam," she said uncertainly.

"It's okay. I'm used to it," Pam told her.

The bell rang. As the boys and girls streamed back into the school, Pam hurried to catch up with Lisa.

CHAPTER THIRTEEN

Blue Lake and Rocky Shore

School was over, Tilly had come to stay and tomorrow she and Janie were leaving for Muskoka. The little car was ready to carry a mountain of belongings. It had a roof-top carrier fixed on top and a trailer, which Tilly had borrowed, hitched on behind.

"And I *still* don't see how you're ever going to get it all in," Mother said, gazing at the equipment piling up in the hall.

Janie had been having the time of her life. She and Tilly had been on a shopping binge. Nobody Janie had ever shopped with spent money in the lavish, unexpected, quixotic way Tilly did. The Chisholms, managing on a bank manager's salary, had to count the cost of everything and plan and save before they could afford any major purchase. Janie would have had her bicycle a couple of years earlier if David had not had college expenses, if Elaine had not had to have her teeth straightened, if Tim had not had to go to the doctor about his allergies, if Dad had not bought a new used car, if the washing machine had not broken down . . . But Tilly had only herself and Janie to worry about. She said she would be paying for the Point for years, but she intended to have a few other things along the way.

Janie followed along, wide-eyed with delight, as they bought sleeping bags, air mattresses, a camp stove and fuel for it, a Coleman lantern, an animal-proof cooler, a tent, a big flashlight, mosquito lotion and spray, jackets with hoods for both of them, rubber boots for Tilly (Janie had a pair). Then Tilly bought an oven! Janie gaped.

"You mean we're going to bake without electricity!" she said.

"Sure," Tilly answered recklessly. "We can do just about anything. Now, what we need next is a closet."

"A closet!" squeaked Janie.

Tilly prowled along the aisle of the department store, looking for a closet. She explained that they would not have room to store much in their tent. If they could just find a closet, a waterproof closet, that would hang in a tree . . .

"Tilly, there's no such thing!"

"That's what you think," jeered Tilly.

And she found her closet. It was really a plastic container which you were supposed to hang up inside your closet in the house, zippered up the front, with shelves for hats.

"Just what we need," said Tilly, and bought it.

The car groaned under the weight of everything they had bought and collected from here and there. Tilly even had a pile of boards in the back and twenty bricks. Janie could not imagine what she planned to build with them.

"Wait and see," was all the satisfaction she got.

They drove and drove. It took nearly three hours. Janie slept part of the way. But when they got into the northern country of rocks and blue lakes, she sat watching every inch of the road, looking for landmarks. Everything looked familiar and yet nothing was quite right until, all at once, they came over the brink of a hill, the car stopped suddenly and then began to inch slowly downward and Janie cried, "Tilly, it's your hill!! We're there!!!"

"Don't distract me," Tilly said between her teeth. "We're not there until I land this trailer safely."

Moments later, they pulled up where they had parked before and there it was—tall trees, sky, blue lake, even the sunset, all waiting for Janie.

"Now we eat!" Janie said happily, remembering the food they had bought, her favorite things—hot dogs, eggs, bacon, chocolate cake . . .

"Now we put up the tent," Tilly corrected her. "If we can," she added.

Janie had had no idea how complicated one tent could be. Tilly had been given instructions, but she had to keep stopping to consult them while Janie stood holding up a side and hoping she was doing the right thing. The mosquitoes whirred around her, nipping at her neck and the backs of her knees. She had no hand free to slap them. It was sheer anguish, but not for one moment did she wish she and Tilly had not come.

At last, it was up. The sun had gone down while they worked but it was still twilight. The bugs were at their worst.

"Cannibals!" Tilly said, swatting two at once.

The tent leaned a little but it was a house just the same. Janie ducked her head and went inside. She sat on the grass and looked out through the open flap. There lay the still lake. Three stars shone in the evening sky. Janie swallowed. It was so beautiful she had a lump in her throat just looking.

"Jane Chisholm, get out here and get to work," Tilly ordered.

They carted the sleeping bags in. Then Tilly brought in her bricks and boards. To Janie's amazement, she built a bookcase right there in the tent. The ground was not quite even but, with a flat stone to help her, Tilly soon had her shelves erected.

Janie was enough her mother's daughter to be taken aback. With all they still had to do, it seemed crazy for Tilly to be putting up bookshelves. Tilly caught the look on her face and laughed at her.

"Listen to me, Stephanie Jane," she said, and there was a serious note under the laughter which Janie did not miss. "I would not live in a place, not even in a tent on my own point, without a place for books. I brought some for both of us. The shelves can hold other things too. Just make sure they don't touch the walls and let the rain in. Here, you can arrange these."

Janie carried in a box of Kleenex, a jar of cold cream, two decks of cards, the flashlight, and three armfuls of books. It was almost too dark to see the titles, but she did make out Eleanor Estes' *The Moffats*, Rosemary Sutcliff's *Warrior Scarlet*, Mary Stolz's *The Noon Day Friends,* Mabel Robinson's *Bright Island*, Frances Hodgson Burnett's *A Little Princess*, Rumer Godden's *Miss Happiness and Miss Flower*, T. S. Eliot's *Book of Practical Cats*, and *The Oxford Book of Poetry for Children*. There were others she did not know. She hugged herself, anticipating the fun before her.

When the car was half unpacked ("Enough for

one night!" Tilly groaned) the two of them crawled into the tent and ate cookies and oranges.

"That was a funny supper," Janie said, "and my hands are sticky."

"Let's go swimming and clean them." Tilly jumped up and began to get ready. Janie gasped and then hurried to catch up.

"You're not supposed to swim right after you eat and you're not supposed to go in in the dark," she scolded, as she skinned out of her clothes.

"Yes, Grandma, I know," Tilly teased. She went on more seriously, "You are right, Janie, but we won't really swim. And it isn't quite dark yet. We'll just go down and paddle in Tim's Cove."

Janie said, "That's okay then."

But secretly, she was a bit disappointed to find out that Tilly was sensible after all.

They splashed each other and shrieked. The water was cold even though it had been a sunny day. There had been a brisk wind and only the surface had been warmed.

"It's a good thing we're the only people up here," Tilly gasped, as she ducked a flying fistful of water Janie aimed at her. "We'd be having a rescue squad out with the noise we're making."

When the two of them got dry, they climbed into their pajamas and curled deep down in the warmth of their sleeping bags.

"This is positively the earliest I've gone to bed in years," Tilly yawned. "But I'm exhausted."

She peered at her watch, luminous in the dark.

"It's not even nine o'clock," she exclaimed.

Janie snuggled deeper into her sleeping bag. She would not go to bed till the last minute, at home, but it was different here. Now, through the tent flap, she could see dozens of stars spangling the reaches of the sky.

"What are Lisa and Company doing this summer?" Tilly inquired.

"Lisa's going to Europe," Janie said, without a trace of envy in her voice. "She talked about it all the time at the end of school. Her Dad is going on a business trip or something. Maybe it's Mrs. Daniels. I don't know. Anyway, they'll be away all summer. They're going to Spain and Italy and I forget where else."

"And . . . Debbie, is it?" Tilly wanted to know.

Janie grinned in the dark.

"She's gone to her cottage with her family. She told everybody she'd kill herself before she'd go—but she went. I saw them go by. Poor Debbie."

"What is the other girl's name?" Tillie probed.

"Pam Potter," Janie said slowly, her laughter dying away. "Pam's just staying home with her aunt."

She told Tilly about Pam. Tilly listened quietly

and completely, the way Tilly always listened. Janie found herself going on to tell of how she and Pam were nearly friends.

"Not like Lisa . . . real friends. Maybe, anyway," Janie finished. "I wish Pam had a Tilly," she added wistfully, after a moment.

"Thank you, Stephanie Jane," said Tilly softly.

CHAPTER FOURTEEN

Dishes and Giant Steps

"Janie! Lunchtime!" Tilly called.

Janie opened her eyes and blinked at the sunlight. She had dozed off again, lying there on the warm bright rocks, with her book open before her. It was such a good book too, but on the island, there was never any hurry. Nobody was going to interrupt her. She had forever to saunter through the story.

"Jan-ie!" Tilly yelled.

Janie scrambled up. The book slid away from her, down the slanting rock. Janie dove for it and caught it before it slipped into the water. Someone was interrupting her after all. Not that she minded. She was as hungry as a hunter.

"Coming, Silly Tilly," she called back—and holding the book high in the air, so that it wouldn't get splashed, she waded back to the mainland.

Tilly had baked raspberry cobbler in her Coleman oven. She rushed Janie through her cheese sandwich so that they could taste her creation. Down the Point from them, men had come to start work on Tilly's "mansion." Janie took each of them a serving of the dessert. They smacked their lips appreciatively.

"Your aunt's a good cook," Mr. Whitman said, scraping the last crumb out of the bottom of the dish.

"She's not my aunt, but I'll tell her," Janie promised.

There was half a floor there now. Janie took a big jump and landed on it.

"I hope you're going to build a step," she said, getting her balance.

"Anything you say, Janie," Mr. Whitman agreed, with a lordly wave of his hand.

Janie stood and looked out through an imaginary window. Tilly had chosen a perfect site. The lake shone before her. Of course, it would be hard to find a place on the Point which was not beautiful, Janie reminded herself.

She hopped down, gathered the dishes and returned to Tilly.

"How's the book?" Tilly asked as they washed the dishes.

"Really good," Janie replied. Then, remembering

herself falling asleep in the middle of a chapter, she looked a bit abashed. Tilly did not seem to notice.

"Janie," she said suddenly, "we've been here over a week. Are you getting bored?"

"Bored?" Janie stared at her godmother. "Me—bored? Of course not! I love it here!"

"I think you really do," Tilly said, half to herself. Then, as though she were answering some question only she had heard, she added, "But I know it must get pretty lonely for you sometimes. Well, your birthday is only two days away now. I have a plan."

Janie said nothing. She was sure she already guessed what Tilly's plan was. Tilly had to go back to Toronto "to fetch it," she told Janie. And Janie was not to come with her. It was to be a surprise.

Janie was as sure as she could be that Tilly was going to get the rest of the family and bring them up for a party. Janie had never been away from home on her birthday before. She had felt queer thinking about it, until she had figured out what Tilly was scheming. She was leaving Janie at the Hollis' farm for the day. Part of Janie wished she could go along. Part of her was glad she did not have to make the long drive. It would take most of the day going down and then coming back. She had wondered why the Chisholms did not just come up in their own car. Tilly's little bug would never hold them all. Then it came to her that Dad probably had to work. Mother had never learned to drive. Perhaps Dad and Tilly would trade cars for a couple of days.

"I hope I'm guessing right," Tilly said now. "There, that's the last. You can dump the water."

"I'll be practically grown-up on my birthday, Tilly," Janie said, coming back with the dish pan.

"You *look* grown-up, I must say," Tilly snorted.

Janie looked at herself through Tilly's eyes. She was brown as an Indian. She had on a skimpy sky-blue bathing suit. She was barefoot. Before she had come north, she had had her hair cut almost as short as a boy's. "Shorter than some!" Mother had said.

But lots of grown women wore bathing suits and went barefoot and wore their hair short. What was it about her that made Tilly laugh at her? Tilly saw her expression and laughed some more.

"Oh, it's not your clothes or your hair, Janie," she said. "It's not even your figure, though you don't have much of one yet, to say the least. It's just you. You look as round-cheeked and big-eyed and freckle-faced as Tim. But I admit you are growing up, bit by bit."

"I am," Janie said, fascinated with this talk about herself.

"Growing up is like playing a game of 'May I,'"

Tilly said. She spoke slowly now, thinking aloud. She was serious. As she talked, the two of them wandered down to the big rock and sat down within comfortable talking distance of each other.

"A game of 'May I!'" Janie was puzzled.

"Well, you take a giant step one day and then, for ages and ages, you just manage baby steps. Once in a while, you even go backward. Then, all at once—and it doesn't happen on a person's birthday necessarily, or even mostly!—you take eight giant steps in a row. Or one of those twirling ones . . . what do you call them?"

"Umbrella steps," Janie informed her. "How about banana steps?"

"They sound slippery," Tilly grinned. "I've taken a few of those. It's a game we all play, you know, Janie. I think I took a giant step the day I bought the Point and became a responsible property owner, all in a minute. I feel quite different."

"You do!" Janie said, frankly astonished. Tilly was Tilly, to her, and always would be. She was a sure thing like the sun in the morning and the stars at night, like the warmth of fire, like the steadiness of earth under your feet.

"Heavens, Stephanie Jane, you make me feel as ancient as Methuselah!" Tilly objected. "I'm still a young thing, comparatively. I've still got years ahead of me to be frivolous in."

"Is that 'growing up?'" asked Janie, her eyes sparkling.

"You stop it! Go away and read your book. I always did think you were an obnoxious child anyway," Tilly said huffily.

Janie laughed and sprawled more comfortably on the rock. Two more days, just two more days till her birthday!

CHAPTER FIFTEEN

A Surprise and a Half

Mrs. Hollis found her standing at the front window for the sixth time that day.

"Goodness, Jane, you'll wear yourself out watching for them," she teased.

"Well, they could be here by now if they'd hurried," Janie said, scanning the empty road.

"Come on out and have some lemonade. I made it specially." Mrs. Hollis was kind. Janie followed her to the kitchen.

Now she was listening. She wished Mrs. Hollis would not be quite so nice. If she would stop talking cheerfully and simply sit and drink her lemonade in silence, Janie might hear the sound of a car turning up the long drive.

It was another hour, though, before they arrived. Janie was back at the window staring at the road with glassy eyes. She was so tired that the car was one-third of the way up the Hollises' lane before she recognized it. It was not Tilly's car at all. It was Dad's.

Janie tore through the house, burst out the door, and flung herself bodily at her family. She had never dreamed she could be so glad to see them. Until they were there, in front of her, she had not had any idea how much she had missed them, even Elaine. Even Rob!

Then Rob grabbed her, upended her over his knee and started delivering her birthday spanking. Janie yelled for help but only Tim tried gallantly to intervene, clutching Rob around one knee and struggling to rescue his sister. When Rob let her go and shook himself free of Tim, Mother moved in and gave her a kiss and a bone-breaking hug.

"And one to grow on!" she said, adding a little pat on the spot where Rob's far from gentle smack had landed.

"She *has* grown, too," Dad commented, looking his daughter over. "She looks taller—and older, doesn't she, Mary?"

Janie did feel older, more sure of herself, more content to be just Janie. But she was not ready to have that discovered by others yet.

"Where's Tilly?" she asked, creating a diversion.

"She'll be along," Mother told her. "She called us this morning and told us where we'd find you."

"You mean . . . *you* aren't the 'surprise?'" Janie said blankly.

"Well, you certainly looked surprised," Dad said. "You didn't think we'd miss your birthday, did you? We aren't part of whatever Matilda is up to, if that's what you mean. Janie, how about taking us to this Point we've heard so much about?"

"Oh, yes!" cried Janie, remembering with delight that none of the family had yet visited the Point. "Come on. 'Bye, Mrs. Hollis. Thanks a lot."

Mrs. Hollis waved. Jim Chisholm turned the car around. Janie took Tim onto her lap.

"Tum left here, Dad," she said importantly, as they reached the end of the lane.

Dad turned obediently. Tim bounced up and down on Janie's knees. She hugged him close. Oh, she was so glad they were here, so pleased to see each of them. . . . But what was Tilly up to?

The Chisholms reached the bottom of the steep hill safely and turned onto the last little stretch of roadway leading to the Point. Elaine was the first to see it.

"Look," she said, pointing. "They've put up a sign."

"We just put it up yesterday," Janie told them.

"Gilead," Mother read. "Where did Tilly get that? Isn't that some place in the Bible?"

"We sing about 'Gilead' in the choir," Elaine remembered. She sang softly,

"There is a balm in Gilead
To make the wounded whole.
There is a balm in Gilead
To heal the sin-sick soul.

"Sometimes I feel discouraged
And think my work's in vain,
But then, the holy spirit
Revives my soul again.

"There is a balm in Gilead . . ."

"That's it," Janie assured her. "Tilly says that this place is like Gilead because there is a balm here too. And Gilead is just the other side of the Jordan River. Tilly says that when you cross the Jordan, you are supposed to reach Heaven—and her point is heaven on earth, so Gilead is its name."

"That sounds like Tilly," Mother said, getting out of the car.

The family trooped over the Point, exploring every nook and cranny. Elaine and Rob splashed over to the island—and Janie did not mind. She had thought she might but it was fun sharing it with them, and in the bright sunlight, it seemed more of a family place—not the special spot, all her own, that it became early in the morning and around sundown.

Suppertime came—and still no Tilly. Mother produced a barbecued chicken, tomatoes, all things Janie loved. And to top it, she even had brought a birthday cake, complete with the seven-minute icing which Janie always demanded. It had candles on top and favors inside. For one dreadful minute, Dad pretended to have forgotten the matches, and then, just as Janie remembered the boxful she and Tilly kept, he produced them.

"Happy birthday to you," the Chisholms sang.

Janie held her breath and tried to think of a wish. She had always wished for a bicycle before, but now, she had her bike. She had this holiday. She had all she could ask for . . . except a friend to share it with.

"A friend," she said to herself and blew hard.

Poof! Every flame went out.

"Wait for us," someone called.

Tilly! The family had been so busy concentrating on Janie and her cake that they had not even heard the car. They jumped to their feet and started up the hill to meet her.

Suddenly, Janie stopped. Tilly was not alone. Getting out of the car, standing uncertainly in the half-light was a girl. Pam!!!

So that was Tilly's surprise! Janie broke into a run.

Amazing, astonishing, wonderful Tilly!

Then, as she neared the car, she saw the third figure climb out.

She halted again, jerked to a stop, unable to believe her eyes.

"Hi, Steffy," said Lisa.

CHAPTER SIXTEEN

Pam Explains

Janie opened her mouth but no sound came out. Lisa was supposed to be in Spain! Lisa was not her friend anyway. Surely Tilly, who understood her better than anyone, knew that much.

Tilly was talking now, covering up the silence with a big hearty voice unlike her own.

"I enjoyed having one girl here with me, so I thought I should have a couple more," she said. "Am I glad you're still here, Jim! I have another tent to put up and Janie and I are not what you'd call skillful at making the things stand erect. I don't suppose you people decided you could stay yourselves, did you?"

"No we can't," Mother shook her head. "We would have been gone before this except we were waiting for you, of course. Rob goes to camp in the morning and Elaine is off to visit Camilla Marriott the next day. I could leave you Tim—but not really. I'd die of lonesomeness without him. Besides, you'd probably get reading a book and let him drown!"

"I would *not!*" Tilly protested.

"Hey, a chipmunk is eating the cake!" Rob shouted suddenly, plunging back down the hill.

Awkwardness was forgotten as they hurried after him. The chipmunk had been only about to begin to eat when Rob spotted him, so they were in time. Janie cut the cake, unevenly to be sure, but everyone got a piece. Dad and Tilly gobbled theirs down and went to get the tent. It was growing dark fast. Pam and Lisa were still only speaking when they were spoken to. They were so polite they made Janie more nervous than she already was.

She even wondered, for one hopeful instant, if she might ask Mother and Dad to take her home with them when they left. Then she knew she could not. Tilly must have had some reason . . . and Pam was Janie's friend.

The tent was up. Janie was hugged. She thanked them again for coming and for her bicycle which was, even though she'd been given it early, her birthday present. Elaine had brought her a book and Rob a new shirt which Mother must have chosen. It was a screaming orange and Janie loved it. Tim had solemnly presented her with a tiny stuffed bear he himself had picked out for her. His eyes were so longing that she asked him to keep it for her.

"What a tactful sister!" Dad exclaimed as Tim crooned over the bear, now his to all intents and purposes.

Then, they were gone. Silence threatened again but Tilly was having no part of it. She got the three girls organized.

"Lisa, you can come in with me," she said firmly. "Janie, you and Pam can share the new tent. Maybe Lisa will sleep in and not waken me at dawn!"

Janie was torn. Lisa taking her place with Tilly! But then, she and Pam were going to be together. Maybe, when they went to bed, she would find out what it was all about.

"I adore sleeping in," Lisa said in her drawly voice.

Janie made a rude face at her back. Pam reached out and touched Janie's arm.

"Don't," she said, so softly only Janie could hear. "Wait till I tell you. Miss Barry's wonderful."

Miss Barry . . . That was Tilly. Janie looked doubtful.

"Okay," she muttered to Pam, "but it had better be good."

"It is," Pam said simply.

"What did you say?" Lisa asked, turning.

"I said 'It's good,'" Pam answered. "Good to be here. I love it already."

"Yeah," Lisa answered, her voice shaking a little. "It's spooky, if you ask me. But I guess it's good too . . . if you like places like this."

Janie could not stand it. What a finish to her birthday.

"Good night," she barked, not looking at anyone in particular. Then she crawled into the tent she was to share with Pam, pulled on her pajamas, determined not to wash her face or brush her teeth, and just lay in her sleeping bag, waiting for Pam to join her or for sleep, whichever came first.

She had not yet calmed down when Pam crawled into the tent.

"Happy Birthday," Pam said.

Happy Birthday! Janie could not say a word. It seemed to her that her birthday had crashed around her. It had been perfect. Tilly had made it so special—and then, there was Lisa. Lisa would hate it at the Point. She had made that clear long before.

"I'd be bored to death in a place like that," Janie remembered her saying.

"Janie," Pam said despairingly, "you're beginning to make me wish I'd never come—and I've been waiting, counting the hours even, ever since Miss Barry's letter."

Janie sat up abruptly. "What letter?" she said. She added, before Pam could answer, "I am glad you came, Pam. I just feel all mixed up. I thought Lisa went to Europe."

"They never ever said they'd take her," Pam said, keeping her voice down. "I think she knew all along they weren't going to. My aunt says that Mrs. Daniels told *her* over a month ago and asked her to keep Lisa for them because their housekeeper was going to take her holiday while they were away. My aunt feels sure they told Lisa then. She says they just decided it all the last minute because her dad realized he wouldn't have any time free to take her around and it would be dangerous for her. She says her mother was worried about her adjusting to the climate too. Every time she talks about it, she tells it a bit differently. But I guess she knows the truth all right. They just plain didn't want to be bothered with her. My aunt says she doesn't blame them."

"I thought they couldn't bear to be without her for even a minute hardly," Janie said slowly, trying to take in this new picture of Lisa.

"Maybe she wishes it were like that." Pam sounded wise. "But Aunt Grace used to work for Mrs. Daniels, you know, before she got arthritis. She used to do typing and stuff. Anyway, she says Mrs. Daniels is so busy it's a wonder she knows she has a daughter. She mostly sees Lisa when she takes her to audition for something and even then, lots of times the housekeeper goes along instead. Her father's really nice. I've met him. I think Lisa gets her niceness from him. But he works all night on that show of his and he sleeps most of the day so she doesn't see much of him either. My Aunt Grace says that Mr. and Mrs. Daniels don't even see each other. That's mainly why they're going on this trip together."

"So Lisa came to stay with you. I'll bet she hated that," Janie said appreciatively.

"She sure did!" Pam agreed with a sigh. "And so did I! But, I kept thinking, it wouldn't be so bad, because Miss Barry's letter came before Lisa did and she invited me up here for a month. I was so excited I couldn't keep quiet about it. Lisa pretended she didn't care one bit. She said awful things about how dull it was going to be up here and how glad she was she wasn't coming. You couldn't make her come even if you dragged her, she said."

"But she's here!" Janie could not follow the chain of events.

"That's what made us late," Pam said.

Janie was getting impatient now. "Late . . . what do you mean?"

"Well, last night, she came into my room. She woke me up—and Janie, Lisa was crying!"

"Lisa!" Janie did not believe it, except Pam sounded so sure.

"Of course, she can act," Pam admitted, paying Lisa a compliment without intending to. "But this was real, I think. She said she could not bear it if I went away and she had to stay there by herself with Aunt Grace. She begged me to ask Miss Barry if she could, please, come too."

"I thought 'wild horses couldn't drag her' . . ." Janie quoted.

"That's what I said. I told her she'd hate it and I wouldn't. But she said she'd never said any such thing, and if she had, it was just because she was jealous, and she kept on and on . . . and I thought of what it's like, alone at home, with Aunt Grace, in the summer. And, well, when Miss Barry came, I asked if she'd mind waiting a minute and . . ."

"You asked her to let Lisa come," Janie finished. She sat still, thinking it over. She added grudgingly, "I guess you couldn't do anything else, Pam. But I still think it's mean and Lisa's going to loathe it here. I know it right this minute. What did Tilly say when you asked her?"

"Well, that was queer, I thought," Pam answered slowly, remembering. "She said 'Lisa, eh? That's not the birthday present I had in mind for Janie exactly.' And then, she said, 'But if there is to be a balm in Gilead, I suppose we must let Lisa try to find it along with the rest of us. If we don't, we'll lose it ourselves.'"

"Oh," was all Janie could find to say.

She slid back down into her sleeping bag and

curled up in the warmth. Pam was shivering. She began pulling off her sweatshirt.

"I wonder, though," Janie thought, looking out through the tent flap at the quiet frosty stars, "if Lisa will want the balm."

"Wear some wool socks to bed," she advised Pam abruptly.

Pam grunted assent and went headfirst into her dunnage bag to find a pair. Janie turned her head to watch her. Then she turned right over, away from Pam, and burrowed into her pillow.

When Dad had said she looked older that afternoon, she had been so sure that she really was. She had felt happier, wiser, nicer.

"One to grow on," Mother had said.

And, later, Janie had thought that that was what this time with Tilly had been—a time to grow on. Talking things over, reading, exploring, dreaming, living away from home, she had felt herself stretching up, getting ready to take the giant steps Tilly spoke of.

She wasn't ready, though. Lisa's coming had showed her that. She was as mixed-up, as hateful as ever. And she wasn't even sure she cared!

"Happy Birthday, dear Janie," she jeered, "Happy Birthday to you!"

She hoped that Pam could not tell that she was crying.

CHAPTER SEVENTEEN

Make Way for Janie

Janie wakened early. The sun had risen but there was still mist lying along the water. She could see that much from inside the tent. Cautiously, she inched out of her sleeping bag and pulled on her boots and her heavy sweater. Pam did not stir. Janie crept out and stood alone, breathing deeply, saying hello to the new day.

But it was still too cold to stay in one place. She trotted up to the privy Mr. Whitman had built for her and Tilly. She smiled when she saw it. She and Tilly, working together, had painted it green. It blended with the trees and bushes around it. Tilly had christened it "The Green House" and, whenever they needed to visit it, they would say casually, "I have to run up to the greenhouse for a moment." Tilly was a lover of even a poor pun, just like Dad.

When Janie came back, Tilly herself was out building a fire. She looked up as her goddaughter came toward her. Her eyebrows raised in a silent question. Then she held out her arms. Janie went to her at once, although she moved quietly, not wanting to waken the other two girls.

"I guess I surprised you, Stephanie Jane," Tilly murmured with a grin. "I'm sure Pam explained."

"Yes, she did," Janie said. She hated to spoil Tilly's morning but she felt she should warn her. "I understand how you couldn't help asking her but, Tilly, she's going to hate it here."

"You don't hate it," Tilly stated. She did not need to ask.

"No, but I'm me. Lisa doesn't like reading much and she does like boys. I don't know what she'll *do!*"

Tilly frowned at the kindling in her hand. Then she gave a quick shrug.

"Wait and see, Janie. Let's give her a chance before we decide for her," she said. "Maybe Lisa isn't as grown-up as she pretends. And maybe I can help her find things to do. How would you like to finish making this fire while I go make a list?"

Janie built the fire carefully as Tilly had taught her. Out of the corner of her eye, though, she was watching her godmother. Tilly stole into the tent and emerged with her clipboard and a felt pen.

With these and some paper, she disappeared to the far side of the Point.

An hour later, Pam and Lisa were up and the four of them had finished breakfast. Tilly still had not mentioned her list. Janie was dying of curiosity but she contained herself.

"Now what do we do?" Lisa said fretfully as the last dish was put away in its orange crate.

"What would you like to do, Lisa?" Tilly asked.

"I don't know," Lisa said. "What is there to do in a place like this?"

"I'm glad you asked me that question," Tilly said smoothly—and produced her list. The three girls studied it. Even Janie's mouth was a little ajar as she saw the possibilities Tilly had dreamed up.

The list read:

Swim
Play croquet
Knit
Play cards
Collect leaves
Pick berries
Hike
Explore woods
Read
Write a letter
Write a book

Sketch
Paint a picture
Play chess
Play tag
Get a tan
Clear out bigger sandy area for swimming
Sing
Climb a tree
Walk to country store (1 ½ miles)
Fish
Learn to canoe
Play Chinese checkers
Sew
Dream

"Gee, Tilly, that's quite a list," Janie spoke up finally.

"It's a start," was all Tilly said. "I'm sure we'll find things to add to it. I'm going to drive around to the Lodge up the lake and rent a canoe this morning. Pam, did you say you can't swim?"

"Yes," Pam said, hanging her head.

"It's nothing to be ashamed of when you haven't had a chance to learn," Tilly told her.

"I have my Senior Swimmer!" Lisa stared at Pam. "I was the youngest one in the class to get it, too," she bragged.

"Were you the youngest person in the class?" Tilly asked quietly.

Lisa nodded proudly.

"And did everyone earn them?"

"Yes."

"Then, of course you were the youngest one," Tilly said briskly. "Pam's going to be the youngest one in my class too. I don't guarantee she'll get her Senior Swimmer but I promise you she'll learn to swim."

Pam glowed. Janie wanted to hug Tilly but restrained herself.

"I have more news for you," Tilly went on. "You all know that I'm an artist."

They nodded. Janie had told them.

"Well, here I am in painter's heaven and I haven't even set up my easel," Tilly complained.

Janie had not once thought of that before. Tilly had seemed so happy, so busy—getting meals, tidying the tent, reading . . .

"I've been housekeeping and having a holiday," Tilly continued, not looking at Janie. "Now I'm going to give up housekeeping. You three are going to get all the meals from now on—and I am going to paint."

For once, they were united. The three of them wore identical dumbfounded expressions. Tilly snorted with laughter. She produced another list. It was horrifying. It listed which one of them was cook, which one did the cleaning up after the meal and which one took care of burning garbage and sweeping out the tents.

"Oh, it won't be that bad," Tilly comforted them. "You'll have lots of time left over to do other things. Besides, it's a lot more fun keeping house outside than in—and much easier too. Now who's coming with me to rent a boat? I think we'll make it a rowboat instead of a canoe. That way, Pam won't be so likely to drown. Till you learn to swim, though, Pam, you'll have to wear a life jacket at all times when you're in that boat and I don't want you to go out in it without me along."

Janie felt breathless. Things were happening so fast she hardly knew what to expect. Tilly was going to paint . . .

Of course, Tilly must have wanted to paint all along. And she'd probably like a tent to herself, too.

"Drat!" Janie said to herself.

She had known that ever since the night before but she had not let herself think it. There was plenty of room in the bigger tent for the three girls. That way, Tilly would be able to read at night the way Janie knew she loved to do.

"Well, are you coming with me or not?" Tilly demanded.

"Yes!"

"Sure!"

They sprang to their feet and were off ahead of her up the hill to the little car.

The boat was not too big for Janie to handle. It was blue. It was an old boat but somebody had given it a new coat of paint and it looked as though it were waiting for Janie to come along and take it for a ride. Tilly made all the arrangements. She got life jackets.

Then she said casually, "Janie, you and Lisa will have to row it home if you want it. It's not far by water, only about half a mile. Here, I'll show you."

She began to point, and then checked herself.

"What am I doing?" she said. "All you have to do is follow the shore and you'll run right straight into the Point. Pam and I will beat you home and have the red carpet out."

"Okay," Janie said.

What else was there to say? Lisa looked longingly at the sleek canoes tied at the dock, but she said nothing. She did not even demand to row. She held onto the sides carefully and made her way to the stern. Janie clambered in after her and sat facing her.

"Don't let her row you onto a rock, Lisa," Tilly said as she and Pam started for the car.

Janie pulled on one oar, turned the rowboat

carefully, and began to row for home. Lisa still said nothing. Her face looked strained, although perhaps it was only the sun shining on the water that made her seem to be frowning.

"Goodness," Janie thought, "this is the only time we've been alone together since that first afternoon when she came over after Sunday School."

That had been only a few weeks before. To Janie, now it seemed years ago.

"Keep out a bit," Lisa advised, "You're getting pretty close to shore. I can see the bottom."

Janie pulled on her right oar. Her arms were beginning to ache. They were not really hurting, just showing her that she needed to row more to build up some muscle.

"There's the Point, isn't it?" Lisa said, as they rounded a curve. Janie looked over her shoulder. She nodded and bent to her rowing again. But she had seen it. It had been just a glimpse, but now she could feel all its beauty, all its wonder, waiting for her. Her island, the island Tilly called hers, lay very still, dreaming and alone, waiting for her. The two tents gleamed in the sun. There were just two, but they gave the Point a gypsy look, as though magical things could happen there.

Two tents . . .

Janie hesitated. Then she thought "Gilead"—

and she began to tell Lisa of her plan. Why couldn't the three girls sleep together in the bigger tent? That would give Tilly room to herself and it would be more fun for them too.

"There's even an extra orange crate we could move our books into," she wound up. By this time, a bookcase seemed as necessary to Janie as it did to Tilly.

Lisa's cheeks flushed. Her eyes brightened. A look, almost an eager look, flashed over her face. For one moment, she was the gay, lovely Lisa Janie had first seen. Then, her expression grew wary.

"That would be okay, I guess," she said listlessly, turning her head.

Janie kept right on rowing. Then Lisa straightened around and faced her again.

"One thing's sure though," she said, "I am a terrific cook. Our housekeeper taught me. I've never bothered with the kind of stuff your aunt has, though. I really cook—you know, pie and . . . and special casseroles. I haven't cooked ordinary camp food. Can you cook?"

Janie returned Lisa's look. In that instant, she knew that Lisa was still Lisa, that no magic was going to make the two of them into kindred spirits, that they were different kinds of people and always would be. She also knew that Lisa could not cook and was afraid to admit it.

A liar. That was what Lisa Daniels was.

It takes one to know one, Janie teased herself, in her inmost thoughts.

Her answer to Lisa, when it came, was spoken quietly, almost comfortingly.

"I'm a lousy cook," she said. "Once I even put sugar in the soup when Mother asked me to salt it. But I can learn—and so can you. Tilly'll teach us both. She'll never let us starve, that's for sure."

Lisa's smile came slowly. It was a new smile, not the gay, self-confident one the old Lisa had worn so lightly. This smile was shy and unsure and real.

"You didn't really put sugar in soup," Lisa said wonderingly.

Janie nodded vigorously.

"I did so," she said. "It was chicken soup, my father's favorite, and he took the first bite . . ."

"Oh, Janie," Lisa said.

Her smile broadened, stretched, grew to a grin. Then she began to laugh helplessly, idiotically. Tears came to her eyes. It was catching. Janie, too, snickered in spite of herself.

When Tilly shouted "Ship, ahoy!" Janie was laughing so hard that she crashed the boat into the shore with a resounding crunch.

"Janie, watch what you're doing!" Tilly shouted, grabbing for the rope.

Pam looked at the two girls in the boat. Their faces were crimson now. Tears had begun to roll down Janie's cheeks.

"What's so funny?" Pam asked.

"She . . . she . . . put sugar in her father's soup," Lisa gasped.

Janie, swaying with mirth, nodded foolishly.

"I did, Pam," she managed. "But I don't really know why it's so funny."

"Neither do I," said Tilly sharply.

She turned, then, in amazement. Pam, too, had exploded into a fit of giggles. She collapsed on the rocks at the water's edge and doubled over, chortling.

"You should just see yourselves," she gasped.

Shaking her head, Tilly left the three of them to it. She thought of the stiff Janie who had climbed into the boat half an hour before, of the unhappy, difficult Lisa who had been her reluctant passenger.

And now, this Janie! This Lisa!

How did she do it? Tilly marveled.

Somewhere, between the lodge and Gilead, Janie Chisholm had taken a giant step.

Tilly felt a sudden sharp longing to tell Janie she had seen the growth in her, not just in that one morning but through all the summer days that led to it. She wanted to let this girl she so loved know, by some special word or look, how proud she was of her at that moment. She hesitated, searching for a way to do it.

The girls' laughter had subsided now. Pam tied the boat securely. Lisa scrambled out onto the rock. Janie followed.

"Here comes the Chief Cook!" she bellowed suddenly, swashbuckling up the rocks toward Tilly. "Make room, Miss Barry. The Chief Cook is approaching. Stand to one side, *if* you please!"

"Make way for Janie!" Pam sang out, following Janie's lead.

Barefoot, wearing nothing but short shorts and a halter top, she managed to sweep along with all the airs and graces of a lady-in-waiting in court dress.

Lisa fell in at the end of the procession. Cupping her hands to form a trumpet, she blew an ear-splitting fanfare.

Watching them come, Tilly knew, all at once, that Janie did not need to be praised. She had discovered, inside herself, freedom and joy.

Janie was still shouting, drowning out the other two with her happy racket.

"Make way! Step aside, lady. Hotdogs à la Janie, coming up!"

Tilly did not say a word. She simply stood back and let them pass.